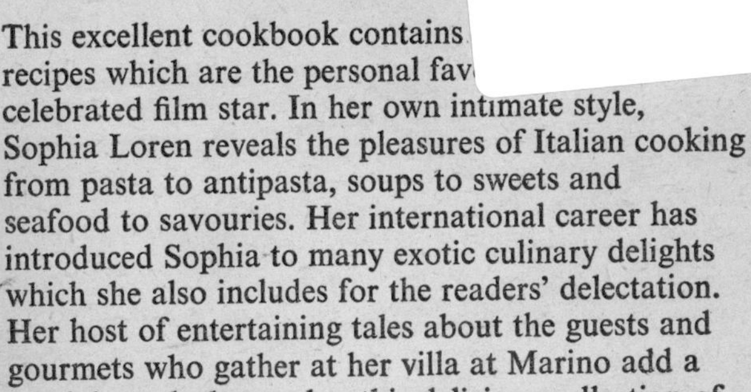

JOIN SOPHIA LOREN IN CRE HER FAVOURITE DISHES

This excellent cookbook contains recipes which are the personal fav celebrated film star. In her own intimate style, Sophia Loren reveals the pleasures of Italian cooking from pasta to antipasta, soups to sweets and seafood to savouries. Her international career has introduced Sophia to many exotic culinary delights which she also includes for the readers' delectation. Her host of entertaining tales about the guests and gourmets who gather at her villa at Marino add a special touch that makes this delicious collection of recipes an added pleasure to use!

Eat With Me

SOPHIA LOREN

SPHERE BOOKS LTD
30/32 Gray's Inn Road, London, WC1X 8JL

First published in Italy under the title
In cucina con amore

First published in Great Britain by
Michael Joseph Ltd, 1972

Published by Sphere Books Ltd 1980

TRADE MARK

Set in Linotype Caledonia

Printed in Great Britain by
Richard Clay (The Chaucer Press), Ltd., Bungay, Suffolk

CONTENTS

PREFACE

Three things are essential in writing a cookery book: time and a love of food and talent for cooking. As regards time, I've always had far too little between films. As for food, the love is only too apparent in the efforts I make to hold back at the risk of losing my figure.

Spring, summer, and autumn 1968. I was in Geneva, a voluntary prisoner of an eighteenth-floor apartment in the Hôtel Intercontinental. The ground fog had blotted out the city and I seemed to be suspended in the sky, in a universe where nobody lived but me. Alone with my great hope which helped me over the boredom of my isolation. The doctors had ordered me to avoid fatigue of any kind, so I focused my whole life upon the only thing that I really cared about: having my baby.

What am I going to do to make the long months go by, I thought. How can I fill up the interminable hours, get the terrible anxiety of waiting out of my mind? With my faithful secretary I began to mess about with getting meals in the kitchen. At first it was for fun but it soon became a daily routine. And then began a period of fantastic gastronomic experiences. I raked through all my childhood memories, the memories of dishes encountered on trips, the instructions of cooks from all over the world, and little by little my notes began to fill up the exercise book I kept in the kitchen. One day when a screenwriter friend had dropped in, he saw my notes and took them to another friend, a writer and also a 'gourmet'. They told me I now had enough material for a cookery book of my own, and encouraged and helped me to prepare it for the publishers. That is how this book came into being. It is dearer to me than any successful film because it takes me back to the nerve-racking days which came to a climax in the birth of Carlo, Jr., the greatest joy of my life.

This book marks my debut into the milieu of gastronomy, but please don't accuse me of hoping to compete with or improve upon the masters of this inspired art. The text I offer you is neither a real treatise on cooking nor a general catalogue of recipes. It is a special book in which I want to suggest the things I like. And in addition to the preparation of particular dishes, it offers personal reflections and reminiscences. A sort of gastronomic autobiography. Yet all my recipes have also been chosen in such a way that they cover all aspects of cooking. If you like the same things I like, this book could be a solution to your cooking problems the whole year round. Apart from an occasional exotic dish discovered during years of travelling, the basic elements of my cooking are typically Italian. I realize that many of the ingredients are difficult to find in shops outside Italy. But I am also aware that there is no large city abroad, in England, Germany, France, or America, where there is not an excellently stocked store of typically Italian products. So, if you want to follow these recipes, it will mean that you must go and track down the ingredients. To assist you in the search, I have included a few hints on alternative and substitute ingredients which should be found easily in any supermarket.

All I can do now is wish you luck in hope that the results will give the right sort of satisfaction and that you will be back for more. This is also a question of personal pride, so I beg you not to let me down. Opening this book is an invitation and a welcome into my kitchen and to my cooking. Eat with me.

OVEN TEMPERATURES AND MEASUREMENTS

	°F.	°C.
Very Slow	250–300	120–150
Slow	300–350	150–177
Moderate	350–375	177–190
Moderately Hot	375–400	190–205
Hot	400–450	205–232
Very Hot	450–500	232–316

Gas Oven Temperatures

Regulo 1	250°F.
Regulo 4	350°F.
Regulo 6–7	425–450°F.
Regulo 8–9	450–475°F

Approximate metric equivalents are:

1 oz.	= 30 grammes
4 oz.	= 114 grammes
8 oz.	= 228 grammes
1 lb.	= 454 grammes
2 lb. 2½ oz.	= 1 kilogramme

Liquid Measures

1 gill	= 0.142 litre
½ Imperial pint (10 fluid oz.)	= 0.284 litre
1 Imperial pint	= 0.568 litre
1¾ Imperial pint	= 1 litre

Antipasti

This opening chapter ought to be called 'fun dishes', which is a broad way of translating the Neapolitan word *sfizio* meaning: the urge to enjoy. Anything *sfizioso* whets the appetite, makes the mouth water, and rouses the spirit of the *bon vivant* who lives in the heart of all Italians. So to begin with we are going to wander through the gastronomical avant-garde before sitting down to the serious courses. These fun dishes that send the taste buds reeling are, at the same time, perfectly simple to prepare. As a lunch or dinner opener we can afford to skip the classical hors d'oeuvre of unquestionable merit, but a little monotonous in its predictable offering of salami and tinned fish which are turned out of their grocer's shop wrappings on to an array of small dishes. My own suggestions, which are intended to seal our friendship in the kitchen, are ideal for meals that are not sit-down affairs formally served, but the thing for summer parties, entertaining around the pool, for example, or in the garden or on the terrace. Besides being delicious, they avoid the risk of upsets or ruin at the transport stage. (None of those famous sauces that end up dripping down the pool umbrella – spattering freshly laundered trousers on their way from the kitchen!) All these are easy to make, easy to serve – and wonderfully easy to eat.

Celery Boats I

Buy some bunches of young, fresh celery, and cut the larger sticks into 'boats' to be filled with the following mixture: Into the electric blender or mixer, put 3 ounces of Roquefort cheese, ¼ pint of milk, and 4 ounces of ricotta (Italian cottage cheese). After blending, turn into a small earthernware dish, add another 4–5 ounces of ricotta, 2 tablespoons of onion purée (or 2 small finely chopped fresh onions), salt, pepper, and paprika to taste, a teaspoon of olive oil, and a few finely chopped pieces of celery stick. The mixture must be beaten vigorously by hand, until it forms a thick paste which is still runny. Put it at once into the refrigerator, and fill the boats at the time of serving. This should be enough for 6–8 people.

Celery Boats II

An alternative filling for celery boats is to beat up the following ingredients in a bowl by hand without using the blender:

3 ounces of tinned tuna fish, 9 ounces of ricotta, one finely chopped medium-sized onion, salt and pepper to taste, and enough milk to prevent the paste from hardening. After filling the celery boats, sprinkle the tops with grated carrot.

Salmon Mousse

The convenience of this recipe is that the ingredients are already prepared. The basis, naturally, is salmon out of a tin: 1 lb. 3 oz. should do for 6 people. Be very careful you get all the salmon flesh without stray bones; then put it in an electric mixer and blend with 2 pints of previously whipped cream. Your salmon mousse is now ready to be spooned into five or six goblets, garnished at the bottom with two or three crisp lettuce leaves. On top you might decorate with a slice of tomato and lemon; or a shrimp or two and a pinch of chopped parsley.

Aubergine Mayonnaise Crostini
(Small pieces of toasted or fried bread)

Roast some large purple unpeeled aubergines on the tray in a quick oven (about 450°F.); 2 pounds is enough for 6 people. When the aubergines look crinkly and the skin has begun to fall away, take them from the oven, cut them open, scoop out the pulp, and leave it to cool. Meanwhile, mix: 2 minced hard-boiled eggs with 2 or 3 teaspoonfuls of onion purée (or a finely chopped onion), then mix these in with the pulp of the aubergines, very carefully, until it has become a smooth paste. Have ready a jar of mayonnaise; mix a good cupful into the paste and stir briskly until it blends smoothly. Then store in a cool place. This cream is then used to garnish little pieces of fried bread (*crostini*) or as an accompaniment to boiled meat, fish, or even hard-boiled eggs.
VARIATION: as this mayonnaise has a very delicate, exotic, and slightly smoky flavour, some cooks add a brilliant touch by mixing in a few pounded anchovies. I personally prefer it without; but try it and see.

Horseradish Crostini

Horseradish, that innocent-looking, fiery little white root which makes tears spring to the eyes of the unwary, is bought whole. Leave it for at least half an hour under cold running water to soothe some of its violence. Then scrape off the rough outer skin with a knife, and, at the cost of a few tears, cut the white pulp into thin little julienne strips. To these add a few drops of vinegar, a teaspoonful of lemon juice, half a teaspoonful of sugar, and mix thoroughly. The mixture is spread over thick slices of dark bread, buttered or not, as you prefer.

Crab and Apple Salad

This is my favourite of the host of combinations I found on the Pacific coast and in the Islands. For 6 people:

Mix about 1 pound of cooked crab meat with enough mayonnaise to hold it together (have both of these ready if you are pushed for time), season with lemon juice, salt and pepper. Then spoon the mixture into goblets with a lettuce leaf at the bottom and put into the refrigerator. Immediately before serving, peel and dice one or two apples, and place a spoonful on top of each portion.

Mushroom and Gruyère Salad

Get some large white mushrooms: wash them well and cut into slices; dice some Gruyère cheese and add to the mushrooms in equal proportions. Mix. Add a few chunks of celery. Please yourself about quantities, but always bear in mind that the basis of the salad must be the mushrooms and Gruyère.

Into a bowl pour some good olive oil with a pinch of salt and a sprinkling of freshly ground pepper: pour the oil over the salad, and stir well. That's all there is to it.

Onion Pâté

Fond of pâté? Try it this way. I'm not suggesting you prepare everything from the ground up. Suppose you have a good pâté ready and waiting in the kitchen – an honest homespun liver pâté, not foie gras. To 9 ounces of pâté, add 3 ounces of Gorgonzola cheese, or a slightly smaller quantity of Roquefort, as it has a sharper taste, and 2 teaspoonfuls of onion purée. Stir well together, making the mixture as smooth as possible. You'll see how much more delicious it is than a simple pâté.

Tuna Fish Loaf

Mix together 7 ounces of tinned tuna fish, a couple of filleted anchovies, a tablespoonful of butter and a few capers. Put it through the meat mincer, then mix again by hand until you have a smoothly blended paste which you then shape into an oval and store in the refrigerator in a bowl well greased with oil. The tuna loaf, now firmly set, is cut into slices to enrich your hors d'oeuvre. At the time of serving garnish each slice with a caper and a circlet of mayonnaise.

Prawn Vol-au-Vent

Buy 6 ready-made (or frozen) *vol-au-vent* (cases), and then about 1 lb. 8 oz. of freshly peeled prawns. Cook slowly in a pan, in a little butter, a few sliced mushrooms with pepper and salt to taste. When the mushrooms are sautéed, add the prawns, leave on the heat for a few minutes longer, adding a few spoonfuls of fish or chicken stock to keep the bottom of the pan runny; then sprinkle in several drops of cognac. Finally mix in a cream made of Béchamel sauce and a beaten egg yolk until it reaches the desired consistency (¾–1 pint of sauce should be about right). If you find this cream of prawns and mushrooms too thick, thin it with a little fresh cream. *Et voilà!* Fill the baked vol-au-vent cases and on each of them place a small slice of fresh tomato.

Neapolitan Crostini

Cut 12 fingers of bread, about 4 or 5 inches in length (2 for each person). On each you place a slice of Mozzarella cheese, 1 or 2 filleted anchovies (according to taste) and some small pieces of fresh tomato. Sprinkle with oregano, pepper and salt; arrange the crostini in a well-greased baking dish; then put uncovered into a hot oven (425°F.) for about ten minutes, and serve at once.

Spiedini
(Cheese skewers)

A Roman trick which always meets with loud appreciation from those unexpected guests who drop in at any time of the day.

Cut slices of bread about an inch or so long, then cut slices of Mozzarella cheese of the same size. Chop a few filleted anchovies. Skewer alternately and tightly the slices of bread and Mozzarella; and between them tuck a few pieces of anchovy. There should be a slice of bread at each end of the skewer. Arrange the skewers in a baking pan well greased with oil; place in a quick oven (450°F.), until the cheese begins to run; at the time of serving ladle up the juice which has collected in the bottom of the pan and pour it again over the skewers

Roquefort Cream

Into an electric blender put 9 ounces of Roquefort cheese and 2 tablespoonfuls of butter; add 2 teaspoonfuls of vinegar, 2 cloves of very finely crushed garlic, the juice of half an onion, a pinch of paprika, and about 1 teaspoonful of finely chopped celery; continue to blend the mixture until it forms a thick, creamy paste. At this point you can soften the paste with a dash of fresh cream. What should result is a creamy blend that spreads easily over fried bread or toast if you want to serve it as an hors d'oeuvre. Or else use it as a sauce for boiled meat and vegetables; it is also delicious on boiled eggs cut in halves lengthwise. That is why I call it my 'all-purpose' cream.

Bruschetta
(Rustic toast)

This is something the peasants still make in some parts of Italy and has a very long history, since bread was the most important food; very often it was the only food for the poor. Even so, as bruschetta, bread is really good. *Allégria!*

It is no more than slices of toasted bread – if possible get those rough brown country loaves that look like millstones, and carve off long slices half an inch thick. In each slice make two incisions in the soft white part so that it toasts well; rub slices with a clove of garlic, to give them the right flavour, season with oil, pepper and salt, and then toast them. This could be an idea for a picnic along with other more elaborate dishes.

Salad of Mozzarella and Tomatoes

I'd like to know who dreamed up this salad, which has become a classic in no time at all.

All you need is Mozzarella (or some other fresh soft white cheese) cut into slices; salad tomatoes, pink and firm, also sliced. A slice of Mozzarella on each slice of tomato – and the salad is practically made. Season with a trickle of oil and a pinch of oregano, or else garnish with a spot of anchovy paste or a few shreds of tuna fish (in which case you won't need the oregano).

Artichokes and Eggs

When you are thinking about serving hors d'oeuvre, the main point lies in the harmonious combination of what goes well or deliciously with what. So remember this dish which is a useful one in any number of situations, from a drink around the pool to a smart cocktail party.

First clean the artichokes very well. This means removing the hard outer leaves and cutting off the spiky ends of the others without, however, reducing them to stumps (if you do you are simply throwing away the most flavoursome part). Force open the centre leaves from the top and cut out the choke with a curved grapefruit knife.

Cook the artichokes according to any reliable recipe; drain.

Hard-boil the eggs, shell them, cut into thin slices or quarters. Then place the artichokes, cut into bite-size chunks, in the centre of a serving dish surrounded by the eggs. Moisten with a light sauce composed of oil, lemon juice, pepper and salt.

Zucchini (Courgettes) *a Scapece*

You can prepare a lot of things *a scapece* (it is a way of marinating food): anchovies, red mullet, other fish, vegetables. But my pick is zucchini a scapece.

You begin by washing the courgettes or baby marrows carefully (allowing about 1 per person), cutting them into rather thin slices, and deep-fat-frying them in a large quantity of olive oil. Then drain them, laying them on porous paper to soak up the oil. When they are cold, put them in a bowl, sprinkle with oregano and add a few mint leaves; sprinkle with a pinch of finely crushed garlic, salt, and, finally, very gradually pour over a few tablespoonfuls of vinegar, so that the marrows are moist without being soaked. Keep them in a covered bowl in the refreigerator or a very cool place, for at least a few hours before serving.

Beans with Caviar

People who pride themselves on being gourmets would decree such a combination well beyond the pale. I can't help finding it a bit odd myself that the lowest of the lowly, the bean (though why it should be considered so in Italy is a mystery. It costs nothing, of course, but is extremely nutritious as well as good to eat) should be combined with the aristocrat, caviar which still trails a cloud of glory as it has done ever since the *belle époque*. But I can't help it. During the time I spent in Russia, I came to adore caviar, and I like it best of all with boiled dried beans. It isn't so strange when you really think about it. All Italians love boiled beans with their tuna fish; so having them with caviar amounts to the same thing, only better. The beans are making an even better match! And there is nothing easier to prepare: dried white beans soaked and boiled till they are soft, then drained and seasoned and each portion topped with a little caviar straight from the jar (I prefer the caviar from the grey sturgeon, but the black, too, with its sharper tang, goes beautifully with beans); add a trickle of olive oil, a pinch of salt, if you really need it, and the job is done. Don't forget to have plenty of buttered toast to go with the beans.

Caponata

This is one of the great Sicilian hors d'oeuvre made from aubergine.

First wash 1 lb. – 1 lb. 8 oz. of aubergines thoroughly, and cut into small squares without peeling; put in a bowl, then sprinkle lightly with coarse salt. Better still, use a colander, because the operation should let the aubergine shed as much of its bitter liquid as possible; and this will take a couple of hours. Meanwhile you can be preparing the rest:

Peel and slice 2 medium-sized onions and fry them in olive oil; add 2 diced ripe tomatoes; a handful of small capers; a few celery sticks cut into small pieces; and a few chopped stoned ripe olives. (These quantities are not rigorously fixed, because Sicilians like to add and subtract ingredients according to the tastes or habits of the family.) Cook a little longer, then remove from the stove. Now take the aubergine and wash in a colander; dry well, then brown lightly in olive oil; when cool, stir into the mixture of onions and tomatoes, etc. Stir *well*, over and over again, then add 2–3 tablespoonfuls of vinegar and a teaspoonful of sugar. Put back on the stove and cook again at a medium heat to reduce the vinegar. Finally you can leave your caponata to cool; and it will be simply *squisita!*

There are people who cling to the ancient style of adding raisins and pine nuts at the vinegar and sugar stage. This is the most complete version. I like the 'classic' version best.

Ratatouille

Whenever I think about the Côte d'Azur, a crowd of delicious memories spring to mind: and one of them is always ratatouille, that marvellous peasant dish from Provence. This is how they taught me to make it.

Take 1 pound of aubergines, wash, then dice. Put in a bowl with a good sprinkling of salt to absorb the bitter juice. This should be done at least three or four hours before you are ready to start cooking. At the right moment, brown a couple of finely sliced onions in olive oil; then add 2 peeled and seeded tomatoes, 1 pound of courgettes, a couple of pimientos, seeded and cut into strips; then the aubergine, after first washing away the salt and drying carefully; a minced clove of garlic (two if you like garlic); a small bunch of herbs (basil, parsley, marjoram, sage leaves); salt and pepper. Let cook at least half an hour until the ratatouille is a good consistency but not too dry.

Spicy Avocado

The first time I went to the United States to make a film, I lived in the magnificent house belonging to the director Charles Vidor, in Beverly Hills. And that's where I made my first acquaintance with that generous fruit, generous to look at as well as to eat: the avocado. The garden was full of them and among the leaves, twenty, thirty, forty avocados would be peeping out each day... so I'd go and pick them. Among the various suggestions and recipes of my American friends I'd always try to pick the best and then add something of my own. And that's how this recipe came about.

The avocado must be exactly ripe, and cut in half. Remove the stone, and in the hollow pour a good teaspoonful of the following dressing: olive oil mixed with vinegar (a few drops is enough, especially if the vinegar is aromatic), salt, pepper, mustard, and chopped parsley. The proportions for the dressing depend much on individual taste. The main thing is that it should be sharp without burning. Once you have added the sauce, put the avocados in the refrigerator and serve chilled.

Neapolitan Fritters

Whenever I start getting homesick in some foreign country I make myself a good dish of *napoletanine*, or

Neapolitan fritters. It's a comforting dish and much less complicated than it sounds.

This is really a sort of stuffed fritter. For the batter, break 6 eggs (for 6 people) into a bowl and mix with 3 tablespoonfuls of milk, 2 tablespoonfuls of flour which have been first smoothed into a paste with 3 tablespoonfuls milk, and a pinch of salt. This batter, a tablespoonful at a time, makes the fritters, which must be almost wafer-thin, practically transparent. As they are fried, arrange them on a piece of porous paper, to drain off the oil.

In the meantime have ready a good tomato purée: 2 crushed garlic cloves cooked 10–15 minutes in 3 spoonfuls of olive oil with a generous portion of tomatoes (2–2½ cups coarsely chopped fresh or tinned tomatoes) and basil and salt to taste; take a good-sized Mozzarella cheese or better still, the milkier smaller *Fior di Latte*, cut into slices or little chunks. Now you stuff each fritter with the Mozzarella, roll it up, and arrange all in a fireproof casserole, very tightly packed. Cover with the sauce, sprinkle with a liberal handful of grated Parmesan, and leave in a moderate oven for half an hour. Serve very hot.

Filet alla Loren

Every so often somebody names a dish after me; it happens to lots of artists. But in this book I wanted to open up my own kitchen for you, so I have tended to skip the dedication recipes. This, in fact, is one exception I'm making, because it has something that appeals immediately to my imagination as well as to my palate.

Guido Furiassi, an authentic gastronomic genius, made it for me in his Milan restaurant, Da Lino.

It is essential to have your beef fillets cut extremely thin and small; for each person calculate 4 slices weighing about 1½ ounces apiece; you will realize now that it is more of an appetizer or hors d'oeuvre than a main course; but there is nothing to stop you from increasing the portion. Besides the meat, you need crumbled Parmesan (not grated), truffles, salt, and olive oil. Have the little table stove ready to cook at the last moment, and fireproof porcelain plates. Now, place 4 slices of the beef on each plate, adding no other ingredients, and put a plate directly on the flame. Then, very quickly, sprinkle over the fillets a pinch of salt, a rounded teaspoonful of crumbled Parmesan, and a slice of truffle. In the time taken for this little operation, the meat will have cooked and the cheese begun to melt. Turn the meat once on the plate, then take it off the flame, and only now pour a teaspoonful of olive oil over the meat. It's fantastic!

Sandwiches

At the utmost, cookery books devote only a very cursory glance to sandwiches. Sandwich making hardly presents a challenge to culinary artistry at the stove. But even here there is room for personal imagination, that special touch which gets away from the usual predictable combinations like chicken, ham, sardines, and so on. And after all, a few well-prepared sandwiches can be a tremendous help at an awkward moment, rushing up a last-minute supper or picnic, or filling in at a party. The whole thing, I insist, lies in getting away from the old tried and true sandwich fillings. Now I'll give you my own formulas. Of course I'm not trying to pass them off as my own creations, but they are the ones which have become my repertory favourites after successful experiment.

MOZZARELLA AND ANCHOVY SANDWICH

On a slice of bread place a slice of Mozzarella cheese about a ¼-inch to a ½-inch thick, and on top a desalted (rinsed) anchovy fillet still moist with olive oil. Cover with the other slice of bread. (This is actually a simplified version of Neapolitan Crostini.)

MOZZARELLA AND PIMIENTO SANDWICH

Cut a slice of bread and cover with a good slice of Mozzarella; on the Mozzarella, place a few strips of roasted pimiento, still moist with their olive oil. Cover with the second slice of bread.

CHEESE SANDWICH

For each sandwich mix vigorously into a paste 1½ ounces of grated Gruyère cheese, the yolk of a hard-boiled egg, enough butter to bind them, ¼ teaspoonful of prepared French mustard, a drop of vinegar, pepper and salt to taste. This filling is best on buttered dark bread.

SARDINE AND CUCUMBER SANDWICH

For each sandwich mix 2 sardines from the tin and still dripping with oil with 1 tablespoonful of butter, ¼ teaspoonful of French mustard, the yolk of a hard-boiled egg, mayonnaise to moisten, pepper and salt. Spread over a slice of bread, then cover with a layer of thinly sliced or chopped cucumber; cover with a second slice of bread.

WATERCRESS AND ANCHOVY-PASTE SANDWICH

You first make an anchovy paste by mashing up some well-rinsed anchovy fillets with enough butter to bind. Spread over the bread and on top put rows of chopped watercress; cover with a second slice of bread.

LETTUCE AND MAYONNAISE SANDWICH

Spread the bread with butter and thick mayonnaise, then place fresh, well-washed lettuce leaves on top. Sprinkle with pepper and salt. Cover.

ANCHOVY AND OLIVE SANDWICH

This time you mash up anchovies and butter with stoned, minced, ripe or green olives. Spread and cover.

SALMON SANDWICH

Mince a good slice of smoked or cooked salmon, mash 2 anchovies with the yolk of an egg. Mix with butter to bind and pepper to taste. Spread on the bread. Cover.

CELERY AND ALMOND SANDWICH

Make a paste of chopped celery, chopped almonds, and mayonnaise. Spread and cover.

MOZZARELLA AND TOMATO SANDWICH

A slice of Mozzarella on a slice of bread covered by a slice of tomato which is still crisp and firm; oregano, salt, pepper. Cover.

CHICKEN AND LETTUCE SANDWICH

Spread the first slice of bread with mayonnaise. On the mayonnaise put a few crisp lettuce leaves; and on top of these slices of roast or boiled chicken. Sprinkle with salt and pepper, and cover.

OTHER CHICKEN SANDWICHES

On the basis of the previous sandwich you can add: slices of tomato, Gruyère cheese, ham, hard-boiled egg – one or more or, if you like a hearty sandwich, all together.

DIGRESSION
(On preparing a dinner)

A little psychology is always useful in preparing for a dinner. Everything will go much more smoothly when you reflect for a moment on the habits, the tastes, and even the curiosity of your guest or guests of honour.

Until relatively recent times, an invitation to dinner implied (among other things) an obligation to exhibit all our wealth, charm, and ingenuity in honour of the guest. The menu was prepared according to inflexible codes, the dishes were as abundant as they were varied and introduced with ceremonial *éclat*. Doubtless they were fabulous meals as far as one can judge from books. I always have the impression of dozens of courses, consisting of dishes which were in themselves a monumental achievement. Today it strikes me that we can, with some advantage, arrange a good dinner on a different scale. This is how I go about it.

First of all, I try to discover what my guests can or cannot eat, the likes and the dislikes. If they enjoy a simple, informal meal, or if they have arrived hoping for something more massive, formal, elegant. Bearing all these facts in mind, I aim for a menu which leaves them satisfied and makes them happy to be there. And then I always try to have at least one speciality which they will not only enjoy, but which will come as a surprise and a discovery. Something, perhaps, which is almost impossible to find at certain times of the year, or a dish which is only made in remote parts of the world, or even of one's own country. If I were entertaining guests in Rome, for example, my Roman speciality would be *penne all'arrabbiata* (macaroni cut on the slant in a fiery chili-laden tomato sauce), or else *carciofi alla Giudea* (deep-fried artichokes as crisp as French fries), or eles a flavoured ricotta. In my forest farm near the Po, a hunting reserve called Tenuta dell'Occhio, I immediately think of roast pheasant if the season is right, or a delicious dish of river eel, and so forth. Something which is not only a pleasure for guests but does honour to the local cuisine; and which, thought about a little beforehand, is not very difficult to make successfully.

Secondly, I always try to include something of my own, because I flatter myself that I am a good cook. Time and again I have tried out all the recipes we have in the house. I have discovered how to vary them a little, adding and subtracting ingredients, to my own taste and giving them a personal touch. And quite often this has met with a chorus of appreciation.

I have a wonderful cook who usually prepares these recipes, but if I really want to show a particular interest in my guests, I like to do at least one with my own hands. Believe me, the moment you are able to say: 'I made this myself, especially for you', you have created a good atmosphere of friendliness and understanding for your guest, at a dinner which might otherwise have fallen flat through shyness or sometimes the inability to 'break through'. Taste, the proper flavour of a meal, is more than a part of the dishes which compose it.

Pastasciutta

There are hundreds of them – I mean it: literally hundreds of ways of cooking *pastasciutta.* I can only give you the ones I have followed myself or else learned by watching my grandmother at home in the kitchen. Some are classics, others not so well known, and some could turn out to be a pleasant surprise. This time, before giving you the recipes, I thought it would be a good idea to list the inflexible laws which govern the cooking of pastasciutta. By now there is no doubt in most people's minds that it is the national dish of Naples, but extraordinarily enough it is not. Or rather it wasn't until two or three centuries ago – as some of you may be surprised to hear. The most common dish of the old Neapolitans was *minestra maritata* (married soup) which was made just as it is still made today, with cabbage leaves and chunks of meat. Now I'll tell you how the change all came about.

The cardinal requisite for cooking pastasciutta is that it must be *al dente,* as we say in Naples, or else it is not pastasciutta. So it is also essential for you to know what al dente means. Al dente means that you can still feel the pasta between your teeth; that you haven't boiled it into a porridge. An al dente pasta, or rice for that matter, blends at once with tomato sauce, with meat sauce, or with any of the other hundreds of relishes that Italian genius for these foods has invented over the centuries. Apart from this it is much easier to digest. This I can assure you from personal experience, and now many dietary specialists are coming around to the same point of view. Not long ago an American magazine wrote that al dente pastasciutta could also be the generating power of that purveyor of erotic vitality known as the 'Latin lover'. I wouldn't swear to the scientific truth of the assertion. But if in doubt, try it and see.

Pastasciutta has a long history. It is eaten in almost every country, and has been known since the Middle Ages, especially in the shape of vermicelli, which is a little thinner than spaghetti. In former times they ate vermicelli much less often than we do. In fact the pasta course only became a daily routine when somebody had the idea of flavouring it with tomato sauce. And the tomato is one of most wonderful gifts that America has ever made to Europe. It took time for the seedlings they first brought to Europe to be properly cultivated. And when it was grown on a widely marketable scale, it turned out that the Neapolitans were the most enthusiastic of all the people of Europe about the tomato. Finally the triumphal day came when an anonymous Neapolitan had the idea of making the famous sauce and using it on his vermicelli. Since then the success has been absolute, overwhelming.

There are books which will give you details of the story and its manifold consequences. Take the problem of the fork. The forks they used centuries ago had only three very long prongs which were no help at all in spearing and twirling the vermicelli and spaghetti. In fact the poor who didn't use forks anyway ate their pasta in their fingers, and so did the nobles as a rule, except at ceremonial dinners. The much shorter four-pronged fork was invented for one of the kings of Naples who so adored spaghetti that he insisted upon having it served at the court banquets. It was more or less the same kind of fork that is used all over the world today.

The Eight Commandments for Cooking Pastasciutta

At this point I would like to put together a number of important rules for cooking pasta correctly. They are all extraordinarily simple operations, but you must observe them to the letter if you want ideal results.

First of all, make sure that you have good-quality pasta made from hard-grain flour. This is very important, not only as regards the flavour but also because you will never succeed in cooking poor-quality pasta the way it ought to be. Pasta made of hard-grain flour cooks consistently all the way through; other qualities do not. Here are the rules that I want to suggest to you:

(1) You need to have a large pot with plenty of hot water in proportion to the amount of vermicelli or spaghetti, so that each string of pasta will cook separately and is free to move in the water without clustering.

(2) The water must be boiling, on a high flame. When it is almost at boiling point (in Naples we say 'when the water trembles') you throw in some salt. But not too much. The water should taste only slightly salty. The reason for adding the salt at this point is to increase the violence of the boiling.

(3) Immediately after, you put in the pasta and turn up the flame. This double onslaught of heat from the salt and the heightening of the flame compensates for the lowering of the temperature of the water when the pasta is added.

(4) As you put in the pasta, spread it out as much as possible, the moment you have increased the heat.

(5) Keep a careful eye on the cooking, and in the meantime have ready a large colander to drain off the water. Don't forget that cooking time varies according to: the quality of the pasta, the composition of the water, the season of the year, and even the height above sea level. The only way to know whether or not the pasta is ready, is to taste a piece. When you feel that there is no longer any trace of rawness, even if it is still firm, have no further hesitation. It is now ready to be drained; with a little practice it will take you no time to judge when to stop the cooking. A few extraordinary people are even able to see when the pasta is ready by looking at it. (But take grim warning: because when pasta starts to disintegrate on the outside while the inside is still hard, it means that it is not of good quality.)

Another warning on the same subject: don't pay too much attention to the cooking time printed on the packet by the manufacturers. Very often this is dictated more by a desire to appeal to average international taste which still is inclined to judge spaghetti by the tinned product, than by a correct estimate for al dente.

(6) An important little secret: before draining the pasta, pour a teaspoonful of olive oil into the pot. It will make the pasta more mobile, which will make it easier to mix with the sauce.

(7) Pour the pasta straight into the colander, which you must shake vigorously to drain off the water, to the very last drop. Two problems emerge if any water remains: firstly the pasta continues to cook and tastes soft and floury; and, secondly, the water dilutes the sauce and ruins the flavour. If you give the pasta a good shaking, both these misfortunes can be avoided. It is not necessary, as some people do, to pour cold water over the pasta to stop it from cooking.

(8) Waste no time putting the pasta into the serving bowl and adding the sauce. It should be brought to the table steaming hot.

And now for the pasta recipes which are my favourites, made in my own way, chosen from the hundreds listed in the books on Neapolitan cooking.

Spaghetti with Tomato Sauce

Nobody ever chronicled the historic meeting between spaghetti, or vermicelli, and tomato sauce, which occurred toward the end of the seventeenth century, and resulted in one of the delights of the Neapolitan cuisine. But I can give you the most orthodox recipe, the one handed down from mother to daughter ever since in every Neapolitan household.

The spaghetti, or vermicelli, must be cooked al dente. Calculate 1 lb. 4 oz. of pasta for 6 people. The sauce should be all ready and waiting the moment the spaghetti is cooked.

Now for the sauce: First pour your olive oil into a saucepan, 3 tablespoonfuls (meagre) for every 2 people; then crushed garlic, one clove for 2 or 3 people. Garlic never fails to put in an appearance in the Neapolitan cuisine, nor in all Mediterranean cooking for that matter. If you find it too strong, reduce the quantity, or do without. But it is a shame! Cook over a lively heat. When the oil is hot and the garlic blanches, add the tomato. For 6 people, with 9 tablespoonfuls of oil and 2 or 3 cloves of garlic you would need *at least* 1 pound of tinned peeled tomatoes, or the flesh of freshly peeled and sieved tomatoes. Add a few basil leaves (using dried basil *only* when fresh leaves are not available); a good pinch of salt (depending on taste and, incidentally, the saltiness of the salt); and a teaspoonful of sugar. These days there is a tendency to forget the sugar, but that is a mistake because it compensates for the acidity of the tomatoes. Lower the flame, and leave it cooking gently for another half-hour. Then it is ready.

When the spaghetti is steaming hot and waiting in a big serving dish, pour the sauce over the top with a generous sprinkling of grated Parmesan (at least a tablespoonful for each person). Stir very well and serve.

Spaghetti with Tomato Purée Sauce

In a large shallow bowl place 2 pounds of sliced firm tomatoes in the earlier stage of ripening, then 2 good-sized onions, peeled and sliced thin; remove the stones from a dozen green olives and chop them and add them in; then add 1 tablespoonful of capers, a good pinch of oregano, a handful or two of chopped parsley, a pair of whole but bruised garlic cloves, and salt and pepper to taste. Cover with olive oil and let stand for 24 hours. When the time is up, ladle up (without heating) the juice which has collected – don't worry about the little pieces of tomato, etc., floating in it – and use it to season spaghetti the moment it is cooked, i.e. al dente; about 3 ounces per person should be ample. Then sprinkle a goodly portion of grated Parmesan over the top.

Spaghetti with Oil and Garlic

This was the ordinary way of eating spaghetti, and vermicelli, in the days before the solemn nuptials with tomato sauce. It should be the simplest recipe of all but there are various versions. First I'll tell you mine, and then we'll glance at the others.

For 6 people cook just over a pound of spaghetti.

Meanwhile you will have prepared the following sauce in a saucepan or pan (a big black iron pan is always the best): 12 tablespoonfuls of olive oil, 6 cloves of garlic cut not too fine, 3 tablespoonfuls of anchovy paste (made by pounding anchovy fillets in a mortar with a few drops of olive oil), freshly ground black pepper, and a handful of chopped parsley. Let it cook for a few minutes; the sauce is ready when it starts to acquire a golden tone, without becoming too dark.

At this point turn the spaghetti, which is now on the verge of being al dente, into the pan and let it cook a few minutes longer, stirring easily so that the sauce is perfectly distributed. Finally, pour it into a large bowl, season with the sharper type of Pecorino cheese, grated, of course – one spoonful per person – and bring it at once to the table.

VARIATIONS:

(1) The same recipe with grated Parmesan instead of Pecorino.

(2) Instead of anchovy use ½–1 teaspoonful (or however much you can stand) of cayenne pepper, or powdered or shredded chilipeppers.

Vermicelli with Mussels

As always the vermicelli must be cooked al dente: 1 lb. 4 oz. for 6 people.

To make the sauce, buy a good 2 pounds of mussels, scrub them well and rinse quickly under the cold tap, then heat them in a tall, covered saucepan. Gradually the mussels will begin to open and liquid run out from inside the shells. When you see that all the shells have lost their liquid, take the saucepan from the fire, remove the mussels and strain the mussel water through a fine sieve into a cup. Now slip the mussels from their shells, and put them in a bowl with a good pinch of chopped parsley.

In a small pan heat 8–10 tablespoonfuls of olive oil with 2 or 3 cloves of chopped garlic and 2 pounds of tomatoes. (If you are using tinned peeled tomatoes be sure you pour the liquid out of the tin first.) Cook for 15 minutes (without using salt!) then add the mussel water and turn up the heat. But wait until the resulting sauce is reduced before putting in the mussels. Let them cook a few moments longer, just enough time for the mussels to lose their raw taste, but without spoiling their consistency and freshness.

This is your sauce for the vermicelli, or spaghetti. You may either pour the sauce over the top, or else turn the vermicelli into the pan, stirring it well in, before serving.

As an alternative to mussels you could use prawns if it is easy to get fresh ones. If nothing fresh is available, however, you would do better to pass on to the next recipe.

Spaghetti with Anchovy Butter

Here is a recipe that always comes as a pleasant and amusing surprise to your guests.

First of all you should make the anchovy butter by slightly softening 3 ounces of butter and mixing it with about 2 ounces of anchovy fillets, with the salt carefully washed away. Pound in a mortar into a smooth, consistent paste, then roll into a ball and keep in the refrigerator until the time comes to prepare the meal.

When you are ready to start cooking, begin by placing 2 tablespoonfuls of olive oil per person into a pan (12 spoonfuls for 6) together with 3 cloves of garlic, bruised but still in one piece. When the garlic has blanched, add 10 ounces of tinned, peeled tomatoes (after throwing away the water from the tin). Mash the tomatoes a little with a fork and leave them cooking for 10 minutes or so, then add a tiny pinch of salt and one of pepper. Take them from the stove and finally toss in a handful of chopped parsley.

Boil the spaghetti, 1 lb. 4 oz. – 8 oz. for 6 people. A moment before straining, place your anchovy butter in the bottom of the serving dish, then pour the carefully strained spaghetti on top; then while it is still very hot, stir well in the bowl so that the butter melts. Now is the time (but you have to be very quick) to throw in the sauce with the fresh parsley, stir for a moment or two, then serve at once. Now for the surprise: this spaghetti tastes almost exactly like spaghetti with mussels, only without the mussels. So you won't want to serve it with Parmesan cheese.

Short Spaghetti with Courgettes

For this spring-like dish you need 2 pounds of baby marrows or courgettes (*zucchini*) to serve 6 people. Wash, dry, cut the courgettes into very small cubes. In 12 spoonfuls of olive oil, fry a chopped up onion and a clove of crushed garlic: when the onions and garlic have blanched, add the courgettes, a few chopped basil leaves, one or two small coarsely chopped tomatoes, but no more; then pour in ½ pint of water, cover the pan, and let cook for half an hour, or even longer until the courgettes start coming apart. At this point, you add 10 ounces of spaghetti, previously broken to lengths of 2 inches, add more water, or better still chicken stock, so that the soup is fairly liquid. When the spaghetti is al dente, the soup is ready.

Spaghetti with Bay Leaves

I met this spaghetti at a friend's house when he gave a dinner to celebrate my Oscar in 1961 for *Two Women*. Instead of offering me a victor's laurel crown, he said he would much rather offer the laurel (known as bay leaves in the kitchen) at the table. I must say his idea couldn't have been better, and I insisted on having the recipe as well.

For 6 people heat 4 tablespoonfuls of olive oil in a pan with a pat of butter; into it slice a good-sized onion, or two medium-sized ones. Cook until the onions look transparent, then add 10 ounces of coarsely chopped, peeled (or drained tinned) tomatoes, a dozen bay leaves, a pinch of salt, a pinch of freshly ground pepper, and ½ teaspoonful of cinnamon. Leave it cooking for ten minutes so that the aromas blend. The result will be a lively and very exotic sauce sufficient for 1 lb. 4 oz. of spaghetti.

Spaghetti with Artichoke Sauce

For 6 people you need 1 lb. 4 oz. – 8 oz. of spaghetti.

You make the sauce with 6 very clean artichokes; tear off the outer leaves and the woody part of the stem. Then remove the prickly ends, cut the artichokes into quarters, and dice the part that remains on the stem. Put all the pieces into a bowl of water into which you have squeezed the juice of a lemon, and soak for about 20 minutes.

Meanwhile, pour into a pan 2 tablespoonfuls of olive oil per person, two or three cloves of crushed garlic and a good handful of parsley. Then heat the pan, add the artichokes, which have been very well drained, and let cook for about 40 minutes until a thickish sauce has formed. Pour over the spaghetti the moment it is cooked. It isn't necessary to add grated cheese.

Spaghetti with Mushroom Sauce

I tried this recipe in the house of a gentleman who was an amateur cook, as well as a self-styled 'beatnik' who liked to let loose his teeming fantasy on the kitchen stove. I've kept it because it strikes me as a very sound formula indeed.

For 6 people heat 8 tablespoonfuls of olive oil in a pan, with 2 or 3 cloves of garlic, bruised but in one piece; 2 or 3 anchovy fillets washed free of salt and minced; 10 ounces of tinned peeled tomatoes (after first pouring the water out of the tin); 10 ounces of mushrooms sliced thin (naturally fresh mushrooms are the best; if you have to fall back on dried mushrooms, you must first 'revive' them in lukewarm water); a pinch of salt, a pinch of pepper and a good pinch of oregano; and, finally, 2 tablespoonfuls of Worcestershire Sauce. Cook them all together for 20 minutes, then turn off the heat and whole the sauce is still bubbling, throw in two handfuls of chopped parsley. This sauce is enough to season 1 lb. 4 oz. of spaghetti.

Trenette with Pesto

Trenette are a type of pastasciutta, long, thin, and flat like little ribbons; they are also known as *linguine* (or 'little tongues'). *Pesto* is a sauce from the Genoa region which is usually served, and rightly so, with trenette. But if you want to try it, bear in mind that you need garlic, a lot of garlic. Today you can find that pesto is often made with only a little garlic in it, or even none at all; but personally I feel that either you do things according to an original tradition, or it is better not to do them at all. After all, there are plenty of other sauces to choose from.

So, for *real* pesto you must pound together (the Italian for 'to pound' is *pestare*) garlic and basil leaves (for 4–6 persons about 3 cloves garlic and 3 cups fresh basil leaves wiped clean with a cloth) and you must do it by hand in a mortar with as much patience as you can command. When the ingredients have settled into a consistent mush, add 5–6 tablespoonfuls of grated cheese – half Pecorino, half Parmesan – until the paste is fully blended with a somewhat oily texture. This is when you begin very slowly to add, drop after drop, a light olive oil (about 5 tablespoonfuls altogether), mixing all the time so that the paste is a little runny, like a sauce. Now it is ready to pour over the trenette or vermicelli, or any kind of pastasciutta (about 1 lb. 4 oz. for 4–6).

Vermicelli with Sauce alla Sofia

Now I'll tell you about my idea for a sauce inspired by pesto. Even if the original inspiration was transformed into something completely different during the process, it is still my own recipe; my friends all say it's good; I hope it isn't just out of politeness, but I don't think so, because whenever I serve it they eat such large helpings and I never know how to go on from there.

Anyway: if you want to try my sauce, pound parsley (instead of basil) and garlic, then add a few well-washed and chopped anchovies, a few stoned ripe olives, a few capers, a thinly sliced onion, and pound and stir very carefully into a consistent paste, to which olive oil is gradually added until the sauce is runny. Use your own judgment as regards proportions, because all the ingredients are flavoursome and get on well together no matter how the quantities are juggled. Now cook your trenette or linguine or vermicelli (al dente, of course), strain well, pour back into the pan for a moment with no more than a few drops of oil, just long enough for the pasta to dry out a little without hardening. Turn into a serving dish, and pour the sauce on top. Serve piping hot and don't forget one last pinch of pepper.

Bucatini alla Matriciana

These should really be called *bucatini all'Amatriciana* because they are the speciality of Amatrice, a town in Latium where the Romans went for their toughest legionaries. As it is a lot easier, though, to say *alla matriciana* that is the usual name of this pasta dish which takes us out of the kitchens of Naples to those of more robust eaters.

You could, of course, use vermicelli and spaghetti alla matriciana, but everyone likes it done with *bucatini*, a fatter edition of spaghetti with a larger hole, which is a good idea as more sauce can get in. There is just one other thing: according to the original recipe, the sauce should be made with *guanciale*, i.e. preserved pork skin treated like bacon. The reason for this is that guanciale has the more delicate flavour: but it isn't easy to find and in the end fat or salt pork bacon does almost as well.

This is how it is made. For 6 people put a tablespoonful of olive oil for each into the pan, then a pat of butter and 5 ounces of pickled pork fat or bacon cut into dice, and 2 or 3 good-sized onions in pieces. When the onions glaze, add half a shredded chilipepper, a pound of chopped tomatoes, fresh or peeled; a few basil leaves, and a little salt. Let them cook for a quarter of an hour. The main thing is that the pickled pork or bacon shouldn't get too hard, which would give the sauce too salty a taste. Pour the sauce over the bucatini and sprinkle it with a generous helping of grated Pecorino. (1 lb. 4 oz. of bucatini for 6 people.)

Spaghetti alla Carbonara

Another Roman dish. Some people may find it tremendously heavy, especially for a first course, but to my mind it entirely depends on your point of view. You only have to see that *spaghetti alla carbonara* isn't just another pastasciutta dish, but a meal in itself. After you have tucked away a good plateful you'll be loaded with enough calories, proteins, carbohydrates, and so on for the rest of the day.

For 6 people, put 1 tablespoonful of olive oil and a pat of butter into the pan; add 5 ounces of bacon or fat salt pork cut into small pieces and a pinch of chopped parsley and let them cook while you beat up 6 egg yolks in a bowl together with 2 tablespoonfuls of light cream or milk and 3 tablespoonfuls of grated Pecorino or Parmesan. Cook 1 lb. 4 oz. of spaghetti (or *penne,* a much shorter, wider, obliquely sliced variety which holds more of the sauce). When the spaghetti is well drained, pour the pork sauce on top, tossing briskly, then mix in the beaten egg yolks. Serve quickly, providing another dish of grated cheese for those who like more.

Pastasciutta with Aubergine

The Sicilians are masters at cooking aubergine. Whenever I go to Sicily I try to eat it in every way it comes.

Now I want to give you a recipe which is among my favourites.

First of all, dice one small aubergine per person without removing the skin, only the seeds. Then fry in a very wide pan (iron, if possible) with a large helping of oil so that it cooks consistently. Some people keep the aubergine under a layer of salt before frying. That is, they place it on a plate, sprinkle a layer of salt over it, then cover with another plate weighted with something heavy on top. In this way the aubergine sweats out much of its bitter juice. On the whole it is a question of taste. Anyway, after the vegetable is fried, it is laid out on porous paper which will absorb the grease, and put away somewhere it will keep warm.

Meanwhile, we come to the second ingredient, the sauce. You make the sauce in a pan, by cooking together 2 tablespoonfuls of olive oil per person, crushed garlic (one clove for 2 people) a pinch of pepper, a few small basil leaves.

Now cook and drain the pasta: bucatini, spaghetti, or rigatoni (the large, fluted macaroni). Pour the sauce on to the pasta with a sharp grated cheese (in Sicily it will almost always be Pecorino); then add the aubergine and serve. It is simply delicious.

VARIATIONS: One variation consists in adding tomato to the sauce; but only a little, otherwise it will overwhelm the taste of the aubergine.

Another more spectacular variation, suggested by a Sicilian admirer, is this one: instead of dicing the aubergine, quarter it, taking good care to leave the quarters attached at the stem (small) end. Then fry it with the quarters still attached (you will need, of course, a very big pan), and it emerges looking like a big, shiny flower. Put one aubergine on top of each plate of pasta (which has previously received its helping of sauce). With the stem ends upward and the quarters pointing down like petals, the aubergines provide very smart hats for your rigatoni or whatever.

Baked Pasta I

This is one of those dishes which immediately bestows an air of festivity on any southern Italian lunch or dinner, because there is such a riot of good ingredients, flavouring, and colours. My guests from every part of the world have adored it – I think probably because it is so flavoursome, the sort of flavours that by some magic put strangers into a warm familiarity with their new surroundings, which in this case is Italian cooking. In short, whenever I have a few guests for lunch or dinner, a baked pasta infallibly works, which is why I made Christiaan Barnard try it when he came to dinner with us at our house in Marino, just outside Rome. He was quite agog with enthusiasm.

For oven-baked pasta you need a pasta type with a rather large hole, to hold the sauces: rigatoni, *mezze zite;* but best of all to my mind is *penne* which is marcaroni-shaped and obliquely cut. Then you will need Mozzarella cheese, basil leaves, tomatoes – a whole list of things. To begin with you make a good quantity of tomato sauce, by heating a few spoonfuls of olive oil in a pan and throwing in a little finely chopped onion. When the onion starts to brown, add the tomato pulp, previously sieved to remove the seeds. You should calculate on 1 tablespoonful of olive oil per person, more or less onion according to taste; and 4 or 5 ounces of tinned tomatoes per person. Cook at moderate heat for twenty minutes, not forgetting a pinch or two of pepper and salt, and ½ teaspoonful of sugar. When the sauce is ready, cut the Mozzarella into thin short slices, let's say one ounce per person; prepare the basil leaves (traditionally Neapolitan housewives rub them clean with a cloth, without wetting them, to keep the aroma, but that is probably asking a bit much in today's kitchen); have ready some grated cheese (preferably Pecorino, but Parmesan will do), breadcrumbs, and finally some fiery sausage cut into small chunks (optional, however, in fact many people find the sausage superfluous as the taste is too strong for the fine blend of flavours, which are complete in themselves).

Now boil the penne or other pasta in a very big saucepan of slightly salted water: (about 4 ounces or slightly less pasta per person). Drain well when cooked al dente, very al dente in this case. Stir in a little of the sauce; then grease the bottom of a fireproof casserole with oil or butter (or best of all, lard, if you have any), and dust with breadcrumbs. Now place half the penne in the casserole, then more of the sauce, then abundant slices of Mozzarella, some small leaves of basil, grated cheese, the chunks of sausage if you decided to use it. Cover this with the remainder of the penne, and pour over the rest of the sauce, a little more cheese, a 'veil' of breadcrumbs on top, and finish off with a few drops of oil or a pat of butter or lard. Put in a hot oven for a few minutes, so that the Mozzarella will begin to melt and bind everything to perfection.

Variations: You can also make three layers of pasta and two of the filling; or else on the top layer arrange half-slices of tomato previously whisked around in a frying pan with a drop of oil; it creates a very eye-catching effect.

Baked Pasta II

For this version of baked pasta you need a type with a large hole in the middle for the filling to penetrate. As in Baked Pasta I, penne are ideal. Then you need a meat sauce (Ragout) (see recipe for Tagliatelle Bolognese Ragout, page 54) and a Béchamel sauce. Make sufficient Béchamel sauce for 1 lb. 4 oz. of penne, by cooking 3 ounces of butter and 3 tablespoonfuls of flour over a low flame, mixing slowly until the flour is absorbed. Then add 1 quart of warm milk, a pinch of salt, and stir until thick and creamy.

Now cook the penne in boiling water. As soon as it is ready, drain, season with a few spoonfuls of Ragout and stir well. Then arrange a layer of penne at the bottom of a fireproof casserole well greased with butter; over the penne spread another spoonful of Ragout, a few spoonfuls of Béchamel and grated Parmesan; put down another layer of penne, then cover with the Ragout and Béchamel as before, and so on until both the penne and sauces are finished. Now straight into a moderately hot oven (400°F.) for about 45 minutes. Take from the oven and wait another half-hour before serving for the penne to cool and the sauces to mellow: this makes it even tastier.

Pasta Omelette

As Pulchinella, Mr Punch's famous Neapolitan cousin, used to say: 'My favourite pasta is when it's fried, pity I never get to eat any.' Then when you asked why, he'd say: 'Because there's never any left over.' Which all goes to show that the Neapolitans have the habit of making these 'omelettes' by using the left-overs from the main meal. But poor Pulchinella is always hungry, he can never lay hands on a spare plate of macaroni or vermicelli, and if he did find one he'd polish it off on the spot. He was right, though, in saying it is a particularly toothsome dish; there are even people today who fry their pasta from choice.

The types used can be macaroni or vermicelli with tomato sauce, or butter and grated cheese, or else a meat sauce. Any of these will do. If you want to cook them especially for omelettes, I would advise a tomato sauce. Once the pasta is cooked, leave it to cool, then mix in a few eggs (one for every 2 or 3 people), and grated cheese. Heat some oil or lard in a pan and pour in the macaroni; as it fries, gradually prod it into a regular shape with a fork, i.e. to form a thick, flat, circular 'cake'. Continue to fry over a moderate heat, taking care that it cooks evenly throughout; this you can achieve by tilting up the pan at the edge, a little on each side, so that the flames won't concentrate on the centre or on only one side.

The 'omelette' is cooked when it begins to form a little brownish crust on the bottom. You eat it tepid, or else cold; it makes a wonderful surprise at a picnic, or if you have a crowd in for cocktails.

Home-made Pasta

Italy still has a matriarchy holding sway over fettuccine, lasagne, or tagliatelle, tagliolini or pappardelle. It is the matriarchy of home-made pasta, a far more ancient and solemn affair than the sun-dried pasta with its little hole inside, like vermicelli, bucatini, spaghetti, and the rest. Home-made pasta is the result of hours of toil spent in blending eggs and flour, and it has been going on since time immemorial (though it started with a far simpler combination of flour and water; the eggs were brought in later to add a note of luxury). But you may be sure that in the days when Naples was one of the great cities of ancient Greece (Magna Graecia) they taught the Romans how to make pasta; there is historical proof. And ever since, in Neapolitan households, a woman who can make proper home-made pasta according to the ancient and glorious tradition has earned for herself a prestige which even today can pass unchallenged.

Fettuccine, Lasagne, and Tagliolini

In my home in Naples we always followed the golden rule of mixing one egg to 3–4 ounces of flour (about 1 cup). For 6 people you should allow 1 pound 6 or 8 ounces of flour (and be sure to use bread or other hard wheat flour). Heap the flour in a mound on a wooden board; then with one finger dig a well in the centre, or perhaps more aptly for Neapolitans, a crater. Into the crater break 6 eggs, both the yolks and the whites (in other parts of Italy only the yolks are used, but at home the rule was always to use the whole egg). After the eggs a very little milk is poured into the crater, about half an eggshellful and no more. When I was a little girl I remember being fascinated by the way the milk was first poured into the eggshell and then into the flour; it was like some sacred ritual to propitiate the household gods.

Now you get to work with your ten fingers and make the flour crater cave in over the eggs and milk, and knead it into a dough. It will be runny at first but as you knead and pound at it, the consistency will thicken as the flour becomes entirely absorbed. At a certain point you will feel the dough getting quite hard and heavy. This is the time for a mighty effort as you work at your heap on the board, flattening it, gathering it back into a ball, over and over again until it becomes soft and elastic, and starts to pull like rubber on the outside. During these efforts it is most important to use the palm of your hands, especially the part at the join of the wrist, as you squash and thin the pasta, then gather it back in your fingers and patiently start again.

As I said before, the pasta is ready when it is well blended and has an elastic feel as though it were alive inside, not just a dead lump in your hands. Now the ball of dough is wrapped in a linen cloth and allowed half an hour's rest. Then comes the moment to roll it out with a rolling pin. This must be done on a pastry board heavily sprinkled with flour to stop the sheet of dough from sticking to the wood or tearing. It stretches wider and thinner at each roll of the pin, and after two or three rolls, it is paper thin. You then fold the dough back on to itself, or roll up like a jam roll and slice every ¼–⅓ inch. You then unroll into long strips of pasta: your hard-won fettuccine. If the strips are narrower you have created tagliolini; if broader (say 1 to 2 inches), we have lasagne.

In all cases cooking follows the precepts of all pastasciutta: an abundance of boiling water, in which the fettuccine (or tagliolini or lasagne) must have ample room to cook without sticking together. The cooking time is considerably less than that of dry or packaged pasta. When a mass of home-made pasta is thrown into the water, it tends at first to sink to the bottom; but after a few minutes it will rise to the surface, and that is the time to take it off the fire, to be thoroughly drained. Fettuccine and tagliolini may be served with abundant quantities of butter and grated cheese; with tomato or meat sauce or, generally speaking, with all sauces used for the dry pastas. Lasagne, however, is served as another sort of dish, as we shall see further on.

Fettuccine in Four Cheeses

Fettuccine have just been described. The moment they are cooked, al dente, turn them into a serving dish, and, for 6 people, cover with 3½ ounces of butter previously melted over a low heat (so that it does not brown); and mix it in well so that every strand of the fettuccine is lightly buttered. Immediately afterwards add ½ pint of light cream, mix again, then stir in the four cheeses: Gruyère, Parmesan, Fontina (a creamy Gruyère type), and mild Provolone; you need about 1½ ounces of each cheese, 6–7 ounces in all, grated or crumbled and already mixed together. Continue the mixing in the serving dish, over and over again, so that the cheeses start to string out and melt, but not completely. Be quite sure they are well distributed through the fettuccine. Serve hot.

Lasagne Pasticciate

All over southern Italy at Carnival time you'll see gigantic mounds of lasagne stuffed full of good things. In this case I have to admit defeat and give up the classic recipe, which is much too complicated; what I can give you is an abridged version which is still delicious. Nor does it really constitute a breach with tradition because this lasagne receives full honours all the rest of the year. It is just that it cuts a rather poor figure at Carnival time.

The lasagne, of course, is the same pasta described earlier only much larger: anything up to 3 inches. Have ready some slices of Mozzarella cheese, a good meat sauce, some sliced hard-boiled eggs, and some meat balls the size of hazelnuts. If the lasagne is for 6 people, the meat balls are made by mixing 4 oz. of minced beef, 4 oz. minced chicken meat, an egg, a pinch of parsley, salt, pepper and about 3 ounces of fine soft breadcrumbs. They must all be well blended, then shaped into balls and browned in a frying pan in hot olive oil.

Now for the assemblage. You put down a layer of lasagne in a pan well greased with butter; top with a few spoonfuls of meat sauce and some slices of Mozzarella. Then another layer of lasagne, then more sauce, then more Mozzarella plus the slices of hard-boiled egg and meat balls. Then you start again with the lasagne, the sauce, the Mozzarella, meat balls, and over them a top layer of lasagne. (You can, of course, build as many storeys as you like of this gastronomic monument.) Over the last layer of lasagne sprinkle a few drops of melted butter (not browned) and bake in a moderately hot oven (400°F.) just long enough for the whole to become compact and firm with a golden crust on top—about 30 minutes.

It goes without saying that this dish is a meal in itself.

Lasagne Verdi Pasticciate

These are very similar to conventional lasagne, except that boiled, beaten, and then sieved spinach is added to the pasta, at the expense of egg. Here is a reliable set of measurements; 1 pound of flour, 3 eggs, 10 ounces of boiled and strained spinach. Then go on to make your lasagne pasticciata as described earlier.

Tagliatelle with Truffles

Tagliatelle are practically the same thing as fettuccine. They differ only in name and the regions of Italy.

In Italy, as in France, truffles are usually eaten sliced thin over some particular dish. But once, when I was in Piedmont, they offered me a plate of tagliatelle that makes my mouth water every time I think of it, with a sauce that put the truffle to a very different use. Just wait till I tell you.

For 6 people melt 2 tablespoonfuls of butter in a pan, adding 3 ounces of Gruyère cut into slivers, so that they will melt easily, and throw in a pinch of pepper and salt. As the mixture is cooking, thin it with a few tablespoonfuls of chicken or beef broth so that it becomes semi-liquid. When all the ingredients are smoothly blended, drop in an ample portion of truffle, either crumbled or chopped into tiny chunks. Stir the truffle into the sauce (two or three times will be enough) and pour generously over a dish of good hot tagliatelle.

Tagliatelle Bolognese Ragout
(*Meat Sauce*)

By now you know what tagliatelle is. But I must admit I am a little shaky about what the orthodox world-famous Bolognese Ragout is. Countless arguments still go on about Bolognese sauce among the master chefs themselves. Every housewife of Bologna is convinced she makes the best Ragout imaginable. And perhaps each is right. But I can give you one which strikes me as very good indeed, even if it isn't the oldest and most orthodox recipe.

Mix 10 ounces of minced beef with an Italian sausage, a carrot, a good stick of celery, an onion, a clove of garlic, a handful of parsley, a few basil leaves, all chopped up but not too fine; put them in a pan over a bright hot flame, with 3 tablespoonfuls olive oil and 3 tablespoonfuls butter. After a while, when the bottom of the pan starts to dry, add a few spoonfuls of broth; turn the heat down a little; and when the mixture looks dry again and begins to acquire a golden colour – calculate 40 minutes – pour in a wineglass of dry white wine and wait for it to reduce; finally put in about 1 pint of sieved tomatoes, either fresh or tinned. Judge your own proportions according to taste; the result should be a good, lively Ragout, but not too red. Leave it cooking over a low flame, until the mixture blends smoothly; then pour it over the tagliatelle (or *any other type* of pasta). This should be enough for 1 pound of pasta, for about 4 people.

Passatelli

This dish is a souvenir of the time I was filming the episode in *Boccaccio '70* and it is a veritable triumph of the cooking of Romagna, a region in central Italy bordering on the Adriatic, which boasts not only an entire population of *bons vivants*, but the heaviest eaters you are likely to find in the Italian peninsula. I still remember with a mixture of terror and admiration the first lunch I sat down to served by the owner of the villa where I was staying: it consisted of an omelette made with 24 eggs, a yard or so of sausage and 2 chickens. What about the waistline, you may well ask? Well, I don't think the battle of the waistline has worried my host for quite some time now.

In Romagna every town, every house even, boasts possession of the genuine recipe for passatelli. Here is the one I always make. For 6 people mix 3 whole eggs, 3 yolks, 12 tablespoonfuls of grated Parmesan, 6 tablespoonfuls of breadcrumbs, a little nutmeg (more or less according to taste), a scant 4 ounces of lean minced beef, the grated rind of a lemon (taking care to grate only the outer yellow skin and not the white pith underneath). Mix everything well into a ball, then put it in a sieve or colander standing over a cloth and press it through (gently but firmly) so that long, spaghetti-shaped sausages emerge, dropping on to the cloth underneath: these are passatelli. Cook them in veal, beef, or chicken broth; they only take a few minutes. Serve with the same broth they were cooked in. However, I have seen the farmers' wives and peasant women cleverly press the passatelli straight through the sieve into the pot.

Tortellini

There isn't a town or village of the Po Valley which hasn't had the honour of bestowing its name on a special variation of those stuffed pasta called cappelletti (little hats), tortellini, ravioli, and so on. The version I like is this one:

The pasta is the same as for fettuccine but it is better

to leave out some of the egg. Two will be enough for 10 ounces of flour (for 6 people). Roll the paste out tissue thin on a well-floured board and cut into circles roughly 1 inch in diameter, using the rim of a liqueur glass (or the special roller kept by the country housewives). Into each circle place a small ball the size of a hazelnut of the following filling: Put 1 tablespoonful of butter into a pan and with it 1½ ounces of calf's brain, 3 ounces of minced fresh pork, and let them sauté a few minutes. Chop into very fine pieces 1 ounce of mortadella, and mix it with the sautéed meats and 1½ ounces of grated Parmesan, 2 or 3 eggs and a little nutmeg. Work at the mixture until it blends smoothly then roll into little balls and place one on each circle of pasta. (It is always best not to start cutting the sheet of pasta until the filling is ready.) Each circle of pasta is then folded over into a half-moon shape; the edges pressed delicately together so that they will stick. These are the tortellini which must be cooked in beef, veal, or chicken broth. They are served in the same broth with an accompaniment of grated cheese. Otherwise, they may be cooked in a large pot of boiling water, carefully drained, seasoned with melted butter and grated Parmesan; or else topped with meat sauce.

Il Rotolone
(*Roly Poly Pasta*)

I don't know why but this name always makes me think of the title of a film: whereas it is really an inspired masterpiece of Italian cooking and one which I absolutely adore.

First of all, prepare a thin sheet of pasta as for fettuccine, but with the addition of slightly more flour:

for 6 people, about 1 lb. 8 oz. of flour and 6 eggs. Then cook 2 pounds of spinach in very little salted water, drain, chop into large pieces, and fry for a minute or two, in a pan with a pat of butter. Lay the spinach on the sheet of pasta, scatter over it small pieces of diced ham (about 5–6 ounces in all) and dust with grated Parmesan; roll it up like a jam roll. This is your *rotolone*. Wrap it in a white linen cloth, and cook it 20 minutes in boiling water in the largest saucepan you have (they sell saucepans especially for cooking rotolone). Remove from the water and unwrap cloth, let rotolone cool a little before cutting it into slices ½-inch thick. Arrange the slices in a tight row on a serving dish, top with melted butter and Parmesan, or else Neapolitan Tomato Sauce.

If topped with butter and cheese, rotolone should be served at once; if you use tomato sauce it is better to heat the rotolone in the oven for a few minutes before serving.

Gnocchi

Gnocchi are part of the Italian tradition of home-made pasta. This is the simplest recipe, which we used to vary the menu with at home.

For 6: boil, then peel, 2 pounds of potatoes, and sieve them; let the resulting purée cool then add 8 ounces of flour and an egg, if you like. Mix steadily and well. When the flour and potato are properly blended, roll into little rolls ¼-inch in diameter; cut them into 1-inch lengths. Finally, with a simple twist of the thumbs, open them a little in the middle. (This helps them to cook better, otherwise they harden inside.) Let them stand on a linen cloth. Then when the moment comes, boil up a big pot of salted water and throw in all the gnocchi, pulling them out of the pot only when they start to float on the surface which means, of course, that they are cooked. Top with a good meat sauce and grated Parmesan (or some other cheese). A last pinch of pepper is also a good idea.

Green Gnocchi

Take a pound of spinach and wash, boil and drain very carefully. This should do for 6 people. Then put it briefly in a pan with a few spoonfuls of olive oil and a clove of crushed garlic. When the flavour begins to rise, chop it fine (after first removing the garlic); add 2 whole eggs and 5 ounces of grated Parmesan. With this you should make the same little rolls as for ordinary gnocchi and cut them into inch-long pieces; boil in a big pot of salted water. They are cooked when they start to float on the surface. Eat them with a good portion of melted butter and grated Parmesan; or with a good meat sauce.

Gnocchi with Gorgonzola Sauce

The gnocchi which I described in the preceding recipes can also be made with a sauce made from Gorgonzola cheese, the Italian cheese similar to French Roquefort or Danish blue.

Gorgonzola gnocchi deserve to be included in the golden album of culinary inspirations. I discovered this idea at Lino's restaurant, in Milan. He served it inside a hollow Parmesan cheese, which not only caught the eye but added to the flavour. Just imagine this sort of little boat arriving on the serving table in front of the guests. The Parmesan cheese rind stands up on its side, hollowed out in such a way that a layer of cheese ½-inch thick remains in the shell. Inside lie the gnocchi in the Gorgonzola sauce with the irresistible smell.

Lino told me that this Parmesan rind is used for a week at the most (every night it is cleaned out and scraped a little). Then it is replaced by another, which of course is only possible in a restaurant where a large quantity of Parmesan cheese is consumed daily. Obviously in a private home you cannot use the same method. But you can at least make the sauce at home.

The gnocchi which Lino makes, however, are a little firmer than those I described above. For example, for 5 to 6 people you use 1 lb. 12 oz. of potatoes, and 6 ounces of flour to which you add 2 eggs. The rest follows the same lines. The ingredients are kneaded together and then you shape the dough into a number of rolls, between ¼- and ½-inch thick. Cut the rolls into little pieces each about 1 inch long then insert your thumb into the centre of each piece and make a dent in it. The gnocchi are ready.

The sauce is relatively easy to prepare. For 2 pounds of gnocchi you melt 2 tablespoonfuls of butter in a saucepan and then add a little less than 8 ounces of the softest and most buttery Gorgonzola that you can find. When the Gorgonzola has melted, add 2 tablespoonfuls of sieved fresh (or tinned peeled) tomato pulp and 7 or 8 tablespoonfuls of juice from a roast of meat or lacking that, beef stock. Cook the gnocchi in boiling water, the same way as for the previous recipe, removing them from the pot when they rise to the surface.

As soon as they are cooked, put the gnocchi into the

saucepan with the sauce, stir very lightly and add ½ pint of thin cream and, for each person, one tablespoonful of grated Parmesan cheese. Even in an ordinary serving dish the gnocchi will be an exquisite treat.
NOTE: if you prefer Roquefort, remember that only 5–6 ounces should be used because the taste is sharper than Gorgonzola. And, for the same reaon, 2 tablespoonfuls of melted butter must be increased to at least 4.

Gnocchi alla Romana

These gnocchi have a more delicate flavour than the others, as will be quickly seen from the ingredients.

For 6 people melt ½ ounce of butter in 1 quart of milk over a low flame; then increase the heat, and when the milk comes to the boil, pour in 7 ounces of semolina, stirring it the entire time; when the mixture thickens and threatens to solidify, pour in another dash of milk; stir again, turn out the fire, add 3 ounces of grated Parmesan, 2 egg yolks, without ever ceasing to stir. When you see that the mixture, now very hot, has a uniform consistency, pour it out on to the marble top of the kitchen table, which you have previously dampened with cold water; shape it into a flat 'cake', about ¼ inch, and leave it to cool. Then with the rim of a glass cut the pasta into circlets: these of course are the gnocchi. To cook them, grease a fireproof dish and dust it with breadcrumbs; lay in it the gnocchi in tight rows each with its edge resting on the next one, cover with melted butter and grated Parmesan, add another layer of gnocchi, then more butter and Parmesan; and bake uncovered in a moderate oven (375°F.) for 1 hour.

DIGRESSION

(*The genuine and the imaginative*)

On this track of psychology, remember that our age must fight for genuine food against dieting and frozen (or packaged) food. When I say genuine food, I must be quite clear about what I mean. We should be grateful, no doubt, to the benevolent manufacturers of so many good things in tins and frozen foods. We have at our disposal food, and very good food it is very often, from any part of the world, every day of the year. They have solved for us the problem of time and labour in preparing meals. But at the same time, it strikes me that this boon of modern science and marketing can make us too lazy for our own good. All too often, tinned or frozen foods make us forget that we can also use fresh material, food which we are able to make with our own hands, even when we have the time and the opportunity to cook.

So when we speak of genuine food, we ought to rediscover the pleasure of cooking and put it before the pleasure of eating; of creating some small masterpiece with our hands, however ephemeral it may be. The advantage of a home-cooked dish of course depends entirely on the freshness of the ingredients and how quickly it can be prepared, but it especially depends upon the love we can put into it and our sense of familiarity with these things.

There was a time not so long ago when women regarded the kitchen stove as an emblem of slavery. Today the slavery is over. So why not transform the chains into an instrument of delight? I know many people who think like that, and many others who only need the right sort of push. Well, here I am to give the push.

Naturally, an evolution, or rather a repression of this kind influences the sort of cooking that you do. Once the great art of cooking lay in transforming the ingredients in a way that went well beyond the natural flavours, the creation of something new, and in the presentation people tried to obtain results which were entirely original. Today we do not have time for such things. Not only has it become impossible in the home, but in restaurants as well. But here, too, I find there is a psychological factor at work, a new mentality which chooses to eat what is natural and direct; that is the traditional dishes which are a genuine aspect of a way of life. And I believe that it isn't a bad thing nor does it mean that we are reduced to an endless diet of beefsteak and salad.

Get your imagination to work in the kitchen, as well as your hands, especially if you have diet problems. What is diet after all? Eating very little or sticking rigidly only to certain foods because you have a liver complaint or are putting on weight is all the more reason why what you do eat should be good. Why be the slave of calorie tables and eat the same old stuff every day when, by exercising a little will-power, you can take yourself in hand and eat everything by knowing exactly when to stop? This is the whole point: you don't have to eat badly, just don't eat so much. You'll lose in the long run. If, however, you are following a prescribed medical regime, you can still make delightful dishes within the quantities and foods you are allowed. The main thing is not to sink into gloom and despondency; don't throw in the towel. One thing I do know is that if you sit down to a bad meal, you leave the table feeling like death and this creates a psychological atmosphere which is a serious threat to your health.

Rice

Like pastasciutta, rice also can be prepared in a hundred different ways. And almost all the ways you can eat pasta are in fact easily transferable to a plate of rice. You can have rice with tomato sauce, meat sauce, mushrooms, courgettes, artichokes, prawns, peas, lentils, and so on. So you are already in possession of a repertoire of recipes from the previous chapter. But at the same time I want to give you a few which are composed exclusively for rice.

Rice Salad

There is a whole list of different rice salads, I know: this one, however, is the authorized version; and ideal for hot summer days.

For 6 people, boil al dente, 1 pound of rice in salted water and afterwards drain carefully. Turn into a serving bowl and mix in 4–5 ounces of tuna fish that has been flaked, 4–5 ounces of diced Gruyère, 4 tomatoes, peeled and coarsely chopped, 2 carrots, also peeled and chopped, a chopped celery heart, 3 ounces of chopped stoned green olives, a handful of chopped parsley and a few chopped basil leaves, 2 hard-boiled eggs, also cut up into small pieces. Mix well, season with a few tablespoonfuls of olive oil, so that the salad is moist rather than swimming, the juice of a lemon, a pinch of salt and one of fresh black pepper. Aferwards, you may decorate the salad with a few slices of a third hard-boiled egg.

Genoese Rice

Fry a good-sized, thickly sliced onion in a large pan with 2 tablespoonfuls of butter and a handful of chopped parsley. When the onion glazes, throw in about 10 ounces of veal, either minced or in small chunks, and 3 well-washed and trimmed artichokes cut into quarters. Meanwhile, have on the stove 1 pound of rice cooking in a good meat broth. When it is half cooked, add rice and broth to the pan and cook over a low flame, giving an occasional stir, adding salt, pepper, and grated Parmesan. When the rice is ready – by now it should be almost dry – pour all into a fireproof dish greased with butter and set it in a hot oven (425–450°F.), until a golden crust has formed over the top. This quantity should feed 6 people nicely.

Rice Pescatora
(Rice with mussels and scampi)

Pour 3–4 tablespoonfuls of olive oil into a black iron pan if you have one, and add a clove of crushed garlic and a carrot and celery coarsely chopped. Wait a few minutes until the carrot, celery and garlic shrivel and yield their flavours, then take them out, and in the same oil cook scampi. For 6 people you will need a good 2 pounds, but they must, of course, be shelled before you put them in the pan, which will appreciably reduce the weight. One thing though: be sure never to salt the scampi or even dip them in flour, but fry them *nature* exactly as they come from the shell; then, when they start to look golden, pour in about ¼ pint of cognac. When the cognac is reduced, after about 10 minutes, pour in the liquid from 2 pounds of mussels which you will have prepared separately according to the recipe for Vermicelli with mussels. When the mussel juice has evaporated, put in the mussels themselves with a handful of chopped parsley and a sprinkling of pepper. Leave them over the heat for another few minutes; in all, cooking time should take only 15 minutes.

At the same time cook the rice in a fireproof casserole. You will need 1 pound for 6 people. First heat the rice on the fire with 2–3 tablespoonfuls of olive oil for 2 or 3 minutes until it has a transparent look, then add a little more than 1 quart of slightly salted boiling water; or better still the same quantity of a lean beef stock; cover the rice and put it in a slow oven. It will take the rice from 15 to 20 minutes to cook, as it absorbs the water or stock. Drain well (you can even tip rice out on to a marble table to make sure no liquid remains) and finally add it to the pan with the scampi and mussels. Stir a little, for 1, 2, or 3 minutes to be sure everything is well mixed; then a last handful of chopped parsley; serve very hot.

Risotto alla Milanese

As far as I am concerned, Milanese risotto is one of the most precious dishes in the world. Everything about it breathes confidence with that flavour of saffron which colours it as gold as the boxes at a La Scala première. It is an exotic taste, a little sharp, but well balanced by all the other flavours. What I didn't expect – when I asked someone for the recipe – was that here too there rages a controversy about ingredients and cooking, which appear to vary from house to house and from kitchen to kitchen. (Another surprise was that in centuries past, they tell me, they actually cooked their risotto in the entrances to the boxes at La Scala, the part where the owners of the boxes leave their overcoats and furs; and they sat down to it in tremendous style at the end of the opera.)

Anyway, this one is probably the most delicious risotto I have eaten, and I have made this recipe over and over again.

Melt 2–3 tablespoonfuls of butter in a pan to which the marrow from a marrowbone and a finely chopped onion have been added. When the onion blanches, add the rice, 1 – 1 lb. 4 oz. for 6–8 people, and cook on a gentle flame as though for a fried dish: that is the whole principle, the rice must not be boiled, but gradually sautéed and moistened with a little broth when necessary (you will need about 1 quart). When most of the cooking is done and the rice is tender, add ¼ teaspoonful of saffron that has first been soaked in about 1 tablespoonful of warm water to bring out the colour.

We are now almost through. When the rice is just about ready (on the whole from 12–14 minutes altogether), season with butter and grated Parmesan. Mix well so that they melt and bind the risotto. Then serve.

Supplì

Anyone who has been to Rome, even if it's only once, will certainly know all about supplìs. They are rice containers stuffed with sauce, minced meat, and Mozzarella cheese. Two or three supplìs will do you just as well as a meal. Or five if you are hungry. Whenever I am filming in Rome I am a great one for supplìs between takes. In southern Italy, and especially in Sicily, they have something very similar called 'rice oranges'. But after experiencing both, I must say I prefer supplìs. They have a livelier taste and are more fun to eat. But here I should mention that the supplìs you are likely to find these days give only a ghost of the idea – if you'll allow me to boast a little – compared to the ones I make from the traditional recipe.

As usual you cook the rice in a big saucepan of boiling water with only a pinch or two of salt: 1 pound for 6 people. Take it out the moment it has reached the al dente stage. First have ready a meat sauce, such as the Sauce Bolognese (included in the recipe for Tagliatelle Bolognese) but it may be easier if I run through this slightly different one here: sauté in 3 tablespoonfuls oil, a cut-up carrot, onion, and celery, and finely chopped garlic clove; then add a scant 4 ounces of minced veal, a handful of parsley, a pinch of pepper and salt; then toss in about ¼ pint of dry white wine; when the wine is reduced, add 1 pint of peeled, coarsely chopped, fresh or drained tinned tomatoes: cook them all in the pan for about an hour and a half.

Now put the rice on a wide, open serving dish, or on a very large plate; strain the meat sauce through a sieve on to the rice, so that the small pieces of meat and vegetables remain behind in the sieve. Then add to the rice three egg yolks and a good handful of grated Parmesan, mix carefully and let it stand – and this is most important – for a couple of hours. Now is the time for you to make the supplì, using your hands: for each supplì pick up the equivalent of two tablespoonfuls of rice (more or less rice according to the size you want them); in the middle put a teaspoonful of the meat and vegetables left behind in the sieve; and add 2 or 3 pieces of Mozzarella, or Fior di Latte cheese which you should have ready on a plate for the final operation. Shape the supplì around this central nucleus: it should be egg-shaped rather than a ball. Cover with breadcrumbs, then drop into an abundant quantity of hot olive oil in a deep pan. Fry them all like this, quickly, because they have to be eaten piping hot. They'll wing you immediately back to Rome, the Rome of those swarming ancient back streets near the Trevi fountain, the Piazza di Spagna, the pulsing heart of Trastévere.

DIGRESSION

(Table manners and smoking)

I always wonder why there should be so many table manners observed today which are quite irrelevant, while we forget about others which should be sacrosanct.

It has always been said that table manners are the fruit of experience, tabulated for our mutual advantage. But of course in time practical circumstances change: the rules remain but they seem like nonsense, at least partly so. Sometimes it is pathetic the way people cling to them; at other times they are downright hampering.

To take some examples: there can be no questioning the advantage of sitting quietly at the table without interfering with or irritating your neighbour or the person opposite. So it is quite reasonable not to make too dramatic gestures in the course of conversation or an ear-splitting noise eating soup or any unseemly noises, for that matter. You ought not to pick your teeth at table, even if toothpicks are misguidedly provided, and so on. These are some of the less pleasant aspects of eating.

It is perfectly reasonable that one shouldn't smoke at the table. Smoking is the most damaging thing there is from the point of view of taste and flavour. The taste of tobacco and smoke spells ruin to the taste buds and prevents you from appreciating flavours. Not only does it disturb the smoker but also his neighbour, even more so. This is really contradicting the majority of people who smoke at table. If you tell them, they get offended, you appear to have said the wrong thing (though in other ways they are perfectly liberal and tolerant people). They say that smoking has no effect on them at all, that they have 'special' taste buds. (Could it be possible that everyone has special taste buds?) The thing I most dislike is that it is usually the women who are the first to light cigarettes at table.

Even the most fervent men smokers usually wait for the women to open the smoking interval during meals. A useful alibi. And the women accept without ever giving this hypocritical homage a thought.

There used to be a time when even the most obsessed smokers didn't dare light a cigarette at table. They put their cigarettes out before sitting down and started again after the meal. Then, I am sorry to say, the United States set a bad example, which spread and spread. The very same people who once were conditioned to forget the urge to smoke at table are the same who today swear they can't resist.

And the wrong of it is that the Americans were the first to realize the harm caused by smoking; hence the anti-tobacco campaign, which is one of the most thriving and effective in the world.

Well, I have made my contribution to this campaign with a very simple proposition: it has been proved that damage from smoking would be considerably reduced if people smoked less and in a more reasonable way. Why not campaign to return to the old custom of not smoking at table? The tobacco companies themselves would support a campaign on these lines, by proposing a truce at lunch and dinner so that one could enjoy a cigarette even more at the end of the meal. And at the end of the meal is exactly the right time: a cigarette or cigar gives much more pleasure, with coffee and brandy. What do you say? Will you join me in spreading the good news and campaign for the restitution of the veto against smoking at mealtimes?

Soups

All the soups I want to suggest are rather different from the run-of-the-mill potages and consommés, because they are much thicker. Very often they are the offspring of holy wedlock between pasta (or rice) and vegetables. I've sometimes been asked why Italians seem to prefer this sort of soup to any other, and I suppose the answer is that all our tastes tend that way. We are so used to pasta and look forward to having something solid between our teeth. Besides I must also mention that these Italian soups of ours could conquer any foreign cuisine – with their combination of natural flavours, and their light but nutritious content.

Cauliflower Soup

Brown a couple of crushed garlic cloves in 3 tablespoonfuls of olive oil, and then at once add a good-sized, well-washed cauliflower cut into pieces and sprinkle with salt and pepper. Let cook for a long time over a low flame, under a lid, until it disintegrates into a mush. Then, for 6 people, cook al dente 1 pound of pasta (the best of all being bucatini); pour the cauliflower over it with an abundant helping of grated Parmesan.

Pasta and Potato Soup

This is the soup of the very poor: but that doesn't mean they don't enjoy eating too.

For 6 people, peel 2 pounds of potatoes and cut into small chunks. In a pan sauté a carrot and tomato chopped up with a few basil leaves and a little olive oil, then add the potato. When you see that it is nearly cooked, add 8 ounces of pasta (here spaghetti is the best, broken into short pieces, or else *cannolicchi*, a large short variety) then at almost the same time, pour 2 quarts of hot water into the pan. When the pasta is cooked and the soup is looking very thick but still runny, it is ready for the table. Season to taste with salt and pepper.

Pea Soup

Sauté together in a tablespoonful of olive oil and a pat of butter for about 10 minutes the following: 4 ounces of bacon or fat salt pork, diced, a chopped onion, a few chopped basil leaves, then add 1 pound of green peas and ¼ pint of stock. Make a thin sheet of pasta as for fettuccine with 12 ounces of flour and 3 eggs, both the white and yolk. Cut the fettuccine very short. When the peas are almost cooked – it should take about an hour – add the pasta, and fill the bottom of the pan with water (1½ pints); wait for the pasta to cook, then serve. Enough for 6 people.

Minestrone

Minestrone is another basic dish of Italian cooking; not only does it change from town to town and from kitchen to kitchen, but it can change from one season to another, even from one day to the next. It would be a mistake to ascribe the phenomenon only to Italian individualism: it still depends on what is available in the way of ingredients according to season and region, because into the minestrone go all the vegetables the cook can lay hands on, with or without pasta or rice. Most famous, perhaps, is the minestrone of Milan (I still remember one *Life* correspondent who called Milan the mother of minestrone) which is such an august dish that its recipe is like Holy Writ. I'll give you my version, and it's really beautiful.

You will always be able to find celery, carrots, and onions the year round, so we shall start with these – 1½–2 ounces of each per person; chop them, brown in a little olive oil with some minced garlic (1 clove to every 2 people). When these first vegetables have acquired that golden look, add to them, depending on the season, a chopped stalk of Swiss chard, some chunks of peeled potato, courgettes (tiny marrows), chopped cabbage leaves, peas, fresh Lima beans and a little coarsely chopped tomato. Then pour in enough stock to cover the bottom of the pan so that the vegetables won't stick, thereby forming a very substantial minestrone. Let it cook like this until the whole becomes soft, like a paste: then it is ready for the table.

Minestrone with Rice, or Pasta

Prepare the minestrone as in the previous recipe; but add much more water or stock to the vegetables. When the cooking is well under way, throw in handful of rice for each person, or short type of pasta with a hole, called cannolicchi. When the rice, or pasta, is perfectly cooked, take the saucepan from the heat and serve.

Pasta e Ceci
(Chick-peas)

For 6 people, soak 2 pounds of chick-peas overnight in 2 quarts of water: the little secret here is to add a pinch of baking soda, which will make them much more amenable in the cooking. In the morning drain the peas, measure the soaking water, and add enough water to total 2 quarts. Boil the peas in the water with a couple of pinches of salt added. After an hour or so when peas are half cooked, ladle out a part of the water leaving only enough to cover the peas. Cook for another hour at least, then add 2 or 3 tablespoonfuls of olive oil, a clove of chopped garlic, half a chopped onion, some minced basil leaves, a cut-up tomato, and a sprinkling of salt and pepper. Cook for another 30 minutes–1 hour and finally the chick-peas will be tender enough to add to the pasta: spaghetti or bucatini broken short or cannolicchi. Now turn up the flame, adding more boiling water if necessary, so that the pasta won't stick. The soup will be very thick, but not too solid. Serve at once. When soup is already on the table in the soup plates add a few drops of crude olive oil and one last sprinkling of pepper.

Pasta with Haricot Beans

For 6 people, chop up half an onion, a celery heart, and a few basil leaves, a clove of garlic with 3–4 chopped rashers of bacon or about 2 ounces of diced salt pork. Fry them in a tablespoonful of olive oil with a pat of butter; then add 2 pounds of dried haricot beans which you have already soaked and boiled, add the bean cooking water and let it all cook until good and soft. At this point add about 1 pint of hot water to the bottom of the pan, and toss in the pasta. This may be some type of dry pasta like linguine or cannolicchi, or else home-made, like fettuccine, cut into very short pieces. In either case you will need 14 ounces. Leave over the heat until the fettuccine or the linguine is al dente; then serve.

VARIATION: You can sieve the beans before adding the pasta, but you will probably have to add more water so that the soup won't stick as the pasta cooks; the soup will have a more delicate taste.

ANOTHER VARIATION, or rather a good hint to make the soup thicker: when the beans are cooked, remove a cup or so from the saucepan, sieve them, and pour this purée back into the soup before putting in the pasta. Obviously you can do the same thing with the other vegetables. Naturally it has quite a different effect to sieving all the beans (or other vegetables). You'll have a *real* bean soup, the genuine article.

Pasta and Lentils

Here the whole dish stands or falls on how you cook the lentils. You need 2 pounds for 6 people. Wash the lentils well; then boil over a moderate flame in 2 quarts of salted water. When they are half done, which should take from 20–30 minutes, draw off some of the water, leaving just enough to cover the lentils, but no more; then add 2–3 tablespoonfuls of olive oil, a pair of cut-up tomatoes, a little basil, and pepper. Throw into the pot a minced pork sausage and a chopped onion which you have previously browned together in a little olive oil. Let the whole lot cook together until lentils are tender. When it is nearing the end, drop in about 8 ounces of pasta (linguine are the best this time) and cook the final round on a bright hot flame, adding more salted water if necessary. The soup must be thick, but not too solid. When you serve it, see that the olive oil bottle is on the table, and add a few drops of olive oil to each plate of soup. You'll be surprised how it brings out the flavour.

Beans with Cotiche
(Pork skin)

Here's a tip for Marcello Mastroianni's fans. If you find your idol is unapproachable, or if he is avoiding you or really is too busy to see you, send him by fair means or foul an invitation for a big feed of beans and *cotiche.* He'll be there in minutes. Beans and cotiche are to Marcello Mastroianni what a snake charmer's pipe is to a snake.

Joking apart, I've always noticed the irresistible appeal of beans and cotiche, especially to men, rather less to women. I still don't know why that should be unless you are prepared to accept the chauvinistic male's answer that a woman's stomach is more delicate than a man's.

Be that as it may, this dish, which is the glory of the traditional Roman kitchen, is solid, and not a little heavy or *grève* as they say in Rome. But that's just what gives it its glamour, the fact that it is a people's dish – substantial.

Cotiche are those irregular strips or chunks of pork skin known as 'crackling' when the animal is roasted. You can buy them at the delicatessen (for 6 people you will need 1 pound); but they take quite a bit of preparation. First of all run them across a flame to singe off any remaining bristle. Then you need to blanch them for a minute or two in boiling water in order to cut them into pieces an inch or so square. Finally you put them back in the pan in a lot of cold water, and cook at a moderate heat. The cooking takes a long, long time, 1–1½ hours, and even when you take them out they are still hard and resistant.

Meanwhile boil 1 pound of haricot beans that have first been soaked overnight, in a big pot full of slightly salted water, containing a sprig of rosemary and a ham bone. The bone should still have the remains of the meat and fat, which are necessary for the flavour.

Now you have the beans and cotiche all dressed up and waiting at the altar. First, however, you should fry in a pan a tablespoonful of minced ham fat, a crushed garlic clove, about 2 tablespoonfuls each of minced basil and parsley, and half a chopped onion. Add to this tinned peeled tomatoes in quantities equal to the beans and cotiche, then sprinkle with salt and pepper. Cook 20 minutes and then add the beans and cotiche and also the meat that has come away from the ham bone, cut into pieces. After another 10 minutes, over a moderate flame, the favourite dish of the Romans is waiting to be served.

Fonduta

This is an equally famous dish and so simple that I have often had to fall back on it in emergencies.

For each person, pour 2 tablespoonfuls of milk and 2½ ounces of soft cheese (the classic cheese is Fontina) into the top of a double boiler. Cook over boiling water until the cheese is melted, then mix in one egg yolk per person. The eggs are already beaten and diluted with half a spoonful of warm milk and a large pat of butter. You mix it all until it blends, with a shining surface. When the fondue is ready I prefer to serve it in individual cups over toast points, according to the old diehard habit in Piedmont. And what could be more splendid than to top it with a good handful of grated truffle?

DIGRESSION
(Table manners, forks and fingers)

While we are on table manners: are we wise in the use we make of knife and fork? Of course, they are extremely useful but sometimes we exaggerate, forgetting that the contact between food and metal (especially if you keep cutting everything and poking and prodding your food on the plate) can spoil the natural taste of the food.

I suppose that sounds strange. And yet everyone can tell the difference between an apple and a pear eaten in the fingers and an apple or a pear that has been peeled and sliced with a knife and fork. The taste is completely different. In the United States some scholars who have conducted experiments have come to the conclusion that in fact small chemical alterations do occur: not dangerous to health but vital to good food.

We all know that it is forbidden to eat fish with a normal knife and fork. This would appear to be one of those unfathomable laws of etiquette. But it has its origins in something quite different: knives give fish a different taste.

I believe that certain fruit, even some cooked food like pizza or a chicken wing or chips, should be eaten in the fingers. There is the question of the change in taste but in certain cases there is also the disappointment by losing the choicest bit, for instance, the crisp baked skin on a chicken wing. For me there is absolutely no doubt that the taste of fried potatoes, for example, begins with the finger-tips. The taste lasts longer, it is more complete because it associates touch and the other senses with the potato.

The moment you pick up some potato crisps with your fingers, you feel this quality at once: the crispness, the salty warmth, the golden feel of the oil. (Forgive the drooling emphasis, but I simply adore potato crisps.)

And anyway what's wrong with eating some things with your fingers? The obvious reply would be: it dirties your hands. But you can always wash them immediately afterwards. And if you are careful, and have had enough practice, you will probably only need to wash the finger-tips and then only one or two. It is just that we aren't used to it. In many countries of the Orient, people still eat with their fingers in the most relaxed and elegant way. The Chinese, of course, eat with chopsticks. But they are children of a very ancient civilization who have handed on so much to European, Western civilization. Have you ever wondered why Arabs and Orientals have adopted so many things from Western civilization in modern times, but have never shown any interest in our way of putting food in our mouths?

It is worth thinking about. In Italy I have read articles and listened to extremely interesting discussions on this point. The fork, after all, is a very ancient instrument. It was already in the news shortly after the first millennium when a Venetian Doge's wife created a scandal by keeping one for her own personal use. There are all those stories of forks used by Catherine and Marie de'Medici at the French court, and so on. But why did their general use only come in so much later, in the eighteenth century, and why was the correct use of the knife and fork such a requisite of the *belle époque*? Because during the *belle époque* an accomplished, if not spectacular, use of the knife and fork was a sure sign of breeding and distinction. A gentleman who could not only peel an orange with a knife and fork but even cut its skin from each of the quarters was considered an undoubted virtuoso. What in fact went wrong in this particular case was a nasty metallic taste in the orange. So I still insist: let us rid ourselves of the tyranny of cutlery whenever we are in danger of ruining the food we eat.

Pizzas

What I am going to say will probably cause grave offence to my fellow citizens of Naples but it is none the less true: the pizza, that most famous pizza of all, is of course beyond any reasonable doubt Neapolitan. And yet, I have eaten excellent pizzas in New York, Nice, and Paris, and (dare I say it?) they are very nearly if not quite as good as those pizzas baking, crisping and melting around the Bay, beneath the shadow of Vesuvius. Now why? On the one hand the Neapolitans might be losing heart to think that this supremacy is on the wane. But on the other hand the knowledge that their pizzas have swept the world should, in my opinion, be a matter of pride. Today the whole world and especially the young are mad about pizzas and pizzerias. A consoling and significant fact: because there is something so elementary, so clean and gay about a pizza, that always it gives me a rush of tenderness towards its addicts.

But you mustn't expect the recipes for classic pizzas in the next few pages. The genuine pizza is only eaten in a pizzeria stocked with a special oven and equipment. What I will give you are recipes for the younger sister of Queen Pizza. Pizzas you can run up in a kitchen without the special pizza baking oven.

Fried Neapolitan Pizza

First of all you must learn to make the dough. Take 1 lb. 4 oz. of flour, 1½ ounces compressed yeast, and as much warm water as you will need. Arrange the flour on the pastry board in the shape of a small conical hill; then dig a crater in the top, and into it put a little warm water in which you have previously dissolved the yeast, and then knead and slam at it energetically for a good half-hour. I'm not exaggerating. You have to bash and punch at that dough over and over again as though it were your worst enemy, squashing it over the board and then hammering at it with clenched fists until it becomes so soft that it almost sticks to your hands. After a good half-hour's toil – adding more water if necessary – roll the dough up into a ball and put it in a soup plate dusted with flour; then cut two slits into the surface to allow the yeast to do its job; and cover with a light cloth.

As the dough rises (it isn't easy to tell how long it takes for the perfect rise; you should regard each lump of dough as a special case; the main thing is that it rises, and that the surface begins to stretch and crack, after which there is no need to leave it any longer), you make the sauce. For this you need a black iron pan if you have one. Put in 1 tablespoonful of oil for each person; crush a clove of garlic for each 2 people. When the garlic is browning, pour in the pulp of 2 pounds of tomatoes, just the pulp, remember, not the liquid, and let it cook over a fierce flame for about 15 minutes. The sauce is now ready. Meanwhile on a row of plates have ready: 10 ounces of fresh milk cheese, such as Mozzarella or Fior di Latte, cut into small pieces; grated Parmesan; finely chopped garlic, and some small young leaves of basil.

Now for the grand finale. Heat a good dollop of olive oil in an iron pan. Then, using your hand (never, never a knife, as you will ruin everything), pull a little of the dough off the ball in the soup plate and shape it into a pizza, round and flat, then fry it carefully in the oil, turning it over quickly: it is better to fry a number of pizzas at the same time if the pan is large enough. In any case, as soon as each pizza is fried, it should be a light yellow colour. Now you spread a spoonful of sauce over it, a little Mozzarella, a little Parmesan, basil, and the chopped garlic. Whoever is eating it should fold it double, being careful not to drop the filling, as the heat of the pastry should still be melting and binding the flavours, as well as keeping the taste deliciously alive. Eat it just like that, in your hands, without any further fuss.

Simple Fried Pizza

The same fried pizzas described in the previous recipe, but flavoured simply with grated Parmesan and basil leaves, are every bit as good.

Pizza with Mozzarella and Anchovy
La Spiziosa

When this pizza is cooked and folded over the filling inside, it is a household equivalent to the *calzone* they make in pizzerias.

Make the dough as for Fried Neapolitan Pizza. As the dough rises, arrange on separate plates: Mozzarella or Fior di Latte cheese, cut into dice or sliced; filleted anchovies washed of their salt and cut into small pieces. At the right moment, pull off your pieces of dough by hand, flatten and round them: on one half put the filling of Mozzarella and anchovy, then fold back the other half of the pizza on top. Press in the edges so they will stick, then cook in the pan of hot olive oil.

Baby Pizzas with Sausage

Another variation on Neapolitan pizza. Same dough, same process. Only this time the filling is made with small pieces of sausage, as spicy as you like it; or else with pieces of sausage and ricotta (Italian cottage cheese); or else pieces of sausage and ricotta mixed with egg yolk. These pizzas are usually made much smaller.

Pizza with Scarola Riccia

A *scarola riccia*, the young frilly lettuce known as Batavian endive (escarole), has the taste of something vital and warm-blooded; for me scarola pizzas are the very best in the world. And most Neapolitans would loudly agree.

You need six small heads of escarole (if you can't find any, use good crisp lettuce instead). Wash them thoroughly but leave them whole, then open the leaves, and stuff the heart with a filling made by mixing stoned black olives, pine nuts, capers, all of them dipped in olive oil and seasoned with salt and pepper. These ingredients should be well mixed in a bowl, one spoonful put in each scarola heart; then close up the leaves again, tie them together with string to avoid accidents on the stove, and cook in a pan with only olive oil at a low to medium heat. When they are well cooked, take them from the fire and allow to cool; this will improve the flavour of the filling.

Meanwhile make the usual dough for fried pizzas. When the dough has risen, cut it into two parts. Press one of the halves over the bottom and up the sides of a well-oiled baking dish; on top of this place 6 escaroles in a row; cover with the other layer of the dough; top with a trickle of oil and bake in a hot oven (425–450°F.) for 30 minutes. When it is done, let the pizza stand for a little to cool off; it should be served tepid, not cold. You'll agree there is no pizza that can touch it.

Pizza with Ricotta

Another variation on Neapolitan Fried Pizza. This time you fill it only with ricotta (you need 14 ounces). Fry and serve very hot.

Baked Pizza I

This one is actually a *focaccia,* a kind of bread made with oil and salt, but it is normally included with the pizzas. You make the same dough as for Fried Neapolitan Pizza, with 1 lb. 4 oz. of flour, yeast, and warm water; then lay the dough, 1 inch thick, in a well-oiled baking dish. Over the dough you spread a sauce made from a few crushed garlic cloves browned in olive oil, 2 pounds of tomato pulp, basil, salt and pepper, which have been cooking together for 15 minutes. Then spread over this a paste of mashed, filleted anchovies (3½ ounces), capers, more basil, and more crushed garlic (but this time only one clove). Put into a hot oven (425–450°F.) for 30 minutes, and the juiciest pizza imaginable is ready for the eating.

Baked Pizza II

You make the dough as for Baked Pizza I; cover it with onions (2 pounds) which have been sliced and fried in oil with a clove of chopped garlic, pepper and salt; then you lay on top of it several slices of fresh tomato, with a few stoned ripe olives, and a few filleted anchovies rinsed free of salt, as well as several strips of pimiento. Bake in a hot oven (425–450°F.) for 30 minutes. This makes a wonderful winter dish as it has the taste of spring.

DIGRESSION
(The large dinner party)

They say that to make a real success of a party, from the point of view of food, you should invite no more than eight guests. You have a fighting chance up to a maximum of twelve, but it's still risky. It is quite true that a dish can succeed only if it is made for a few people but I have always maintained that this rule is due to something quite different which has nothing to do with cooking. Try to sit with more than eight people at table; the conversation runs into the sand. Everyone ends up by addressing the person to his right or left, especially if the table is rectangular and not a round one. Not to mention official dinners with the guests all wedged together on only one side of the table!

I have given this matter a lot of thought. But I must say that even the fork supper system, the substitute for large dinner parties (where you have to eat standing up, balancing an assortment of food which you would never otherwise have chosen, mixing flavours and textures, juggling forks, plates, glasses, casting furtive glances in all directions to avoid being pushed, and having your feet trodden on) is uncomfortable. I just don't like it. There was a time when it struck me that cocktails were a brighter form of entertainment. But now I am convinced that the game isn't worth the candle. I have looked for another solution.

How then can a large number of guests be reconciled with a good table, having everyone sitting down to eat, with all of them sitting there in a row like dummies in a shooting gallery instead of seeing and talking to one another?

Here is what I do. If there are more than twelve guests (obviously up to this number I put them all at the same table whether it is round or not), I seat them at different tables so that everyone can be comfortable. But I don't have them served at the table. Everyone helps themselves at the buffet with the aid of the staff; then he or she sits down where he wants to beside whomever he or she finds most interesting. When the course is finished, somebody clears away the plates and cutlery but the guest can go straight back to the buffet for another helping. Then he goes back to his old place or somewhere else so that he can talk to other people.

I tried this once and I carried on with it because I see that my guests are happy with the system. They have the advantage of a sit-down dinner, and the advantages of a cocktail party or a reception where full freedom of movement is possible.

Naturally if there are elderly people present or guests of particular distinction, you can always ask them what they would like to have brought to the table so that they don't have to move. But generally speaking, people are only too glad to get up and change places. At all events, there are waiters constantly wandering among the tables, serving wine, waiting for requests. So I repeat, the essential is not so much to reduce the service as to give more freedom to the guests.

There is another advantage in the presentation of the menu. A few guests may be fussy about what they eat, but for most of them you require the simplest food and the most convenient if they have to carry plates and glasses in their hands. With my system, it is less risky to bring hot dishes, or ones with sauce, to the table: you can thus give free range to the imagination.

Corn Meal

Whenever I eat sweet corn as corn flakes or popcorn in the States, I always wonder why they never use *polenta* on that side of the Atlantic; in the Old World in days gone by it was a great way of filling up cheaply. Today it still remains a humble peasant dish, but delicious when it is made strictly according to the traditional recipes. History tells us that sweet corn was the mainstay of the Aztecs and Incas; and that the first colonials who landed on the coast of Virginia found enormous comfort from maize when they grew it under the instructions of Pocohontas. I've also been told that when Columbus's sailors set foot for the first time on the island of San Salvador they found the Indians roasting corn and were most unfavourably impressed. An opinion which was to be shared by others in Europe, where the new product was only used as fodder for livestock. Then there came a time when famine stalked the land and men decided that corn was better than nothing, and from then on a brand-new gastronomic experience was born.

In Italy corn is almost entirely used as a meal; with the meal something between a dough and a batter is made. Its name is polenta and it can be eaten with sauces, sausages, roast meat, milk, cheese, fish, and so on; it fits in everywhere.

Polenta

For all Italians, especially in the north, polenta rouses memories of Alpine peaks, impressive landscapes, vast fir forests, and mountain trails. I shall tell you how I was taught to cook polenta at Cortina d'Ampezzo, that beautiful winter resort where I sometimes go for my holidays.

First you need a large saucepan; and it will make all the difference if it is copper. For a good solid portion of polenta (enough for 6 persons) you boil 2½–3 pints of water with 2 teaspoonfuls of salt; then sprinkle in 1 lb. 4 oz. of yellow corn meal, taking good care that it doesn't lump, and that the water doesn't stop boiling even for a second (the best way is to turn up the heat when you sprinkle in the meal). When the meal is all in the pot, you must begin to stir with a wooden spoon and keep stirring without stopping for a moment. Housewives say it is best to stir in one direction without ever reversing, but personally I don't really see that it makes much difference. At the same time you should have a second pot of water on to boil.

After a quarter of an hour, sprinkle in another 8 ounces of the yellow meal and about ¾ pint of boiling water; but make sure that you are stirring at the same time; you will notice now that the polenta is thickening, so that every now and then you should add a tablespoonful of boiling water so that the polenta doesn't lump (you will need to add about ¾ pint altogether). After half an hour, you will notice that the polenta has reached the proper consistency, which is thick but mobile, and comes easily away from the side of the pot. It is cooked. But for the perfect flavour you need to work at it with the wooden spoon for another half hour. This is the only problem with polenta. In all it takes at least one hour of hard labour (but you can of course hand the spoon over to somebody else); worth it, though, because in an hour and a half it will have reached sheer perfection.

When the cooking is done, turn the polenta out on to a wooden board. You can slice it with a piece of string rather than a knife; and anoint the pieces with butter or fresh soft cheese, and grated Parmesan. You can add sauces of all kinds because, as I said earlier, polenta goes with anything. But now I'll give you some special recipes which I've tried during my travels through Italy.

Polenta Crostini

Make a dish of polenta, as described. Spread the polenta about ½-inch thick over a wooden board. Cut into slices approximately 1 x 2 inches. These measurements are not all that important. What does matter is getting conveniently shaped strips of polenta to toast under the grill into little golden slabs which shouldn't be too brown. Butter each piece while still piping hot, then put a spoonful of scrambled egg on top, and you may like to finish it off with a piece of anchovy and half a stoned olive. If you have the polenta already made at home, Polenta Crostini make a wonderful supper snack after the theatre.

Polenta Crostini with Kidney

This may sound rather a complicated dish, but I can assure you it is worth every second of the time required; I found it among the recipes of that patriarch of Italian cooking, Luigi Carnacina, and it soon became one of my 'specials'.

Make the polenta as before. Wait for it to cool, then cut it into disks 3–4 inches in diameter (slices will do just as well, but the discs make it more spectacular; you can please yourself). Meanwhile, cut three veal kidneys of approximately 8 ounces each in half lengthwise (later you can put them together again with toothpicks to preserve the shape). Cut out the spongy gristle inside, then sprinkle with pepper and salt, cover with olive oil and and leave to marinate for an hour or so, turning them over from time to time.

When the time comes to cook the kidneys, grill them under a moderate heat for not more than 15 minutes. Meanwhile, dip the polenta discs lightly in flour and fry them in olive oil until they become crunchy and crisp. Finally put half a kidney on each polenta disc, and serve. Enough for 6 persons.

Polenta with Gorgonzola

Make the polenta as before. When it is properly cooked, pour half on to the wooden board and shape into a round, then cover with a filling composed of 8 ounces of Gorgonzola cheese well mixed with 4 ounces of butter. As you are spreading the filling, make sure you leave a ¼-inch border around the edge of the polenta. Now pour the rest of the polenta over the top of the filling, pressing the edges together and shaping the whole into the form of a dome. Then put it into a hot oven (about 425°F.) for two or three minutes so that the cheese, the butter inside, melt and soak into the polenta. Serve in slices (enough for 6 people). It is perfectly delicious and I am deeply grateful to some Milanese friends of the Academy of Italian Cooking, who gave me this dream of a recipe. (As in the case of gnocchi, if Gorgonzola isn't available, French Roquefort will do just as well.)

Polenta Pie

Prepare your polenta as directed. In this form the polenta will emerge a little less solid than usual. The moment it is cooked, take it from the fire, and, without turning it out of its saucepan, mix into it a series of ingredients: six hard-boiled eggs (sliced); 8 ounces each of bacon and sausages; the bacon is diced and browned in 2 tablespoonfuls olive oil and drained, then the sausages are fried in the same oil and chopped up after being cooked. After these ingredients are stirred into the hot polenta, pour all into a well-oiled baking dish, sprinkle the top with the oil left in the sausage and bacon pan, and then put into a hot oven (425–450°F.) until the top becomes a golden crust. A robust dish, as nobody would deny. But you'll be horrified at how much of it you can eat. Enough for 6 people – maybe.

DIGRESSION

(The eye wants its satisfaction too)

An old Italian saying which refers to food because the way the food is arranged and dressed has its importance.

A dish is first appreciated by its smell and then by the way it looks, then the taste, as we all know. In fact, a real expert has only to take a sniff and a glance to see whether the dish has turned out well or not. Certain smells can whet the appetite amazingly. But you don't need a proverb to tell you that; it is only too obvious. For the visual aspect, we have the proverb I quoted at the beginning. But the visual aspect doesn't stop at the way the food is arranged. The table, too, is important. The way it is prepared, the choice of tablecloth and napkins, the plates, the cutlery – to coax desire to eat what has been cooking in the kitchen.

Decorating a table is important, and it is not easy. It isn't just a question of making it groan with all the plate and silver we can lay our hands on, but the way the decoration ties in with the food. A country lunch, for instance, is hardly for refined, embroidered tablecloths, napkins, and good china plates, or vice versa. An embroidered or lace tablecloth, crystal glasses and silver cutlery do excellently for the *suprêmes*, the *bourgognes*, the *relevés* of a great chef: a nice, rough linen cloth, peasant wine goblets and wooden handled knives and forks are the thing for thick soups, cold meat and roasts, eaten out of doors.

I know some of this is really cliché, but in one's actual experience the principle isn't always so easy to apply; it is a question of taste and sense of proportion and backing good taste before ostentation.

There are one or two other observations I would like to add. We are speaking of toning the table to the food, but we must not forget or undervalue the fact that the table must also be

Sophia surrounded by fragrant green vegetables and prepared salads (Photo Soldati)

In her kitchen in New York, Sophia has prepared a tasty risotto with aubergines (Photo Secchiaroli)

For salads and minestrone soup Sophia insists on a variety of the freshest greenstuffs
(Photo Secchiaroli)

In the kitchen of her Marino house, Sophia prepares the pasta dough for fettuccine (Photo Soldati)

toned to the guests. You think out the most subtle menu to keep your guests happy: the decoration should also play its part.

I have noticed so often that a small detail is enough to spoil everything, just as it can give that ineffable 'right tone'. It is enough to think about it a moment or two. For example: the guest may be from a foreign country, so on the menu you have something which reminds him of home. And on the table too there could be a souvenir of his home town: a certain kind of glass, a salt cellar, a tablecloth and napkin, some little knick-knack which will soothe him psychologically in the atmosphere of a dinner abroad.

Fish

I hope that some of these fish recipes come as a discovery and a pleasant surprise. They all belong to a highly varied tradition from different parts of the world. So there is something for everyone.

In conservative menus, the fish course always follows the soup and after it comes the entrée, before the main meat dish. Today a breath of freedom and a wider acquaintance with the process of diet and digestion have overthrown the ceremonial of the dinner table and fish have come into its own as a main course, rather than something sneaked in, or a fanfare for other courses. Naturally I am now referring to everyday meals – because that is the main purpose of this book. We can leave ritual for banquets and/or formal gala dinners where there is no problem about waistlines and where the menu is governed more by considerations of prestige and spectacle than the digestive capacities of the guests. On these occasions, when and if you are called upon to face one, it is still axiomatic that the fish course will come before the meat.

Roast Fish alla Fiamma

A good-sized fish, e.g. a *dentice* (bass) or *orata* (porgy or dorado) both excellent Mediterranean fish, roasted plain on an open grill, cannot be bettered. But there are always times when you feel you would like something a little different. Here is an idea I discovered during a weekend on the coast of Sardinia. While the fish was on the grill, somebody was busily preparing to serve it and I took careful note of everything.

You take a large plate covered with salt; and on top of the salt sprinkle a layer of herbs: first rosemary, then wild fennel; thyme, parsley, borage, marjoram; whatever there is. As soon as the fish is done, lay it on the bed of herbs and smother it with another layer of the same herbs. Then dash a little glass of cognac or rum, whichever you prefer, over the fish. Get it alight, wait for the flames to die, and brush the burnt herbs away. It's magic.

Spiedini alla Marinara

Spiedini (skewered food) comes in every imaginable form, shape, and size. But have you ever thought of this one? Scampi (or Dublin Bay prawns), squid, cuttlefish and porgy or other boned fish? Clean them all very carefully, and cut them so that the pieces of each fish are all roughly the same size and can be threaded on to skewers. Then warm 3–4 tablespoonfuls of olive oil, a crushed clove of garlic and a few chopped sprigs of parsley and brush on the skewered fish as it roasts on the open grill. Takes only a very few minutes – time enough to catch the smoky taste of the fire without losing the tang of the sea.

Skewered Oysters

Remove the oysters from their shells and wrap each one in a very thin slice of pork fat. Now the oysters can be threaded on to skewers: say 6 oysters for each skewer, and 2 skewers for each person. Dust with a little salt and put on the grill. Cook for three or four minutes then serve on small squares of buttered toast spiced with a pinch of red pepper.

Fish Salad

A fish salad that never fails is composed of the meat of boiled fish and crustaceans: orata (porgy), sea bass, *cernia* (a kind of perch), rock lobster, crabs, or scampi (Dublin Bay prawns). Scoop out the white flesh of the various fish and crustaceans, dice it (but not too small), then put it in a large serving dish, mix with slices of hard-boiled egg, peeled and diced boiled potatoes, diced pickled cucumbers or quarters of crisp pink tomato, small capers, and chopped parsley. Bind the salad with mayonnaise and it is ready. It is always wise, however, to let it stand a little while in the refrigerator in a mould. Better still in a mould lined with gelatine so that when the salad is turned out on to the serving plate, it is neat and compact under a gelatine glaze.

Polynesian Fish Salad

I love Polynesian salad where the fish is marinated in salt without ever coming into contact with a fire. This is the way I learned to make it when I was out in the Pacific.

Choose a good-sized porgy, bone it, and dice it. Now let it marinate for a couple of hours with one or two spoonfuls of rock salt, according to size. Then wash the fish well to eliminate the salt; arrange it on a serving plate and cover with thin slices of onion, grated coconut, peeled and seeded quarters of lemon, lemon juice, and very thin slices of hard-boiled egg. These should all be arranged alternately, one beside the other. Now sprinkle everything with a pinch of pepper and a generous dash of coconut milk. Then leave it to marinate for 30 minutes in the refrigerator before serving.

Lobster Cocktail

My first encounter with lobster cocktail, which is one of the simplest delicacies of American cooking, was in 1956, when I was in Madrid. Its godfather was Cary Grant, of whom I was a very shy but adoring admirer. (It was the time I was making my first American film with him, and in English). The new taste of lobster cocktail, as new as the new world that I was then making my professional way into, was one to which I took an instant liking. It comforted me, and when you are young and shy and confused, there is no better comfort than something really comforting to the stomach. Cary was giving that great warm grin of his – I'll never forget it – beaming with all the pleasure of a host initiating the unfledged guest to a new speciality. The smile was comforting too. It was the beginning of our friendship. So I have never been able to regard lobster cocktail just as something you sit down to and eat. For me, in its absolute, disarming simplicity, it has always carried the taste of loving friendship.

Here is the way I was taught to make it:

You want about ½ cup of lobster meat per person, boiled and diced. Then for the sauce, put one egg yolk for every 2 people, lemon, salt, pepper, paprika, all well blended, then a tablespoonful of ketchup for each person, a drop of Worcestershire Sauce, a few drops of cognac, and a spoonful of light cream. Mix all these together and when they are properly blended, put in your cubes of lobster. Portion it out into glass cups, each with its lettuce leaf at the bottom, and garnish with small capers and slices of gherkin. The glass cups should be served on plates or in small silver basins, surrounded with crushed ice. The temperature, in fact, ought to be only a few degrees above freezing: the golden rule for all good cocktails.

Fish Baked in Beef Stock

The world of good eating is full of surprises. One evening in a restaurant in Milan I had the most exquisite oven-roasted fish, cooked to a Sicilian recipe which the writer Vincenzo Buonassisi had unearthed in his travels and restored to a place of honour. I owe the recipe to the kindness of this good friend and writer (the restaurant called this dish after him as it met with such fantastic success). However strange it may seem today, in the old days it was a perfectly normal way of cooking fish.

In Italy the habit of mixing meat and fish in the same pot lasted right through the Middle Ages, and also in France; and it persisted through the Renaissance when certain stews were still bolstered up with beef stock, even if the stew happened to be fish.

Moreover there is nothing difficult about making it. First you should find a good-sized fish: a bass, porgy, or sea perch. Slit it open on one side, just enough to cut away a little of the flesh from the backbone; a good tip which allows the fish to cook uniformly. Then place it in a big baking dish, douse it with good-quality olive oil, cover with sliced onions, and fill up the rest of the space with cooked potatoes, either sliced or in chunks. Now you can finish off by adding a pinch of salt, capers, some chopped black olives, pieces of octopus or prawns. Put it in a very slow oven for 35–40 minutes and at intervals (this is the secret) moisten the fish with beef stock. It should turn out perfect. The taste of the fish is brilliantly emphasized and the potatoes deliciously enriched by the combination of flavours.

Rock Lobster with Port

A classic this one, and especially fine if you have a big fat lobster and can cook it in pieces rather than whole. First I fry butter, chopped onions, and carrots, then put in the pieces of lobster and continue the cooking over a fierce flame, adding salt and pepper, and turning the pieces over from time to time. When they are on their way I pour in light cream until everything is covered. Then I leave the mixture for 20 minutes on a low flame. At this point I transfer the pieces of lobster to a serving dish, letting the sauce cook a few minutes longer as I add a pat of butter and whisk it into a froth. Finally I add about ¼ pint of port, put the sauce through a strainer, then pour it over the lobster. If you go in for refinements, rearrange the pieces of lobster on the serving dish to resemble its original shape.

Sardines a Beccafico

This is a Sicilian dish I am simply crazy about. First of all because sardines (which we call *blue sardine* in Italy because of the blue scales and flesh) are extremely tasty whether they are fried or baked; but especially in the way I am about to describe, known as warbler style (called after those little birds much appreciated by gourmets). As there is such an abundance of sardines, and they cost so little, many people are inclined to snub them, but I don't agree. Those people are missing out sadly.

Slit the sardines in half through the belly, leaving them intact down the back (as you also do for frying); of course you will want to cut off the head and remove the long backbone; wash the sardines, and after separating them, open them flat like a book and leave them to drain.

Meanwhile prepare the filling: for each pound of sardines heat in a pan 4 tablespoonfuls of olive oil with 3–4 tablespoonfuls of breadcrumbs. When the breadcrumbs are crisply fried, put them in a bowl and mix in a tablespoonful of sultanas (carefully washed and dried), a tablespoonful of pine nuts, a handful of chopped parsley, a pair of washed and chopped anchovy fillets, and a dash of pepper. Mix them all thoroughly but with not too heavy a hand. Then scoop out a spoonful of the paste and spread it on the open sardine which you then roll around the filling so as to form an *involtino* (little roll), and spear with a toothpick to hold it together. Repeat the operation for each sardine. Finally you put them all into a well-oiled baking dish; another sprinkling of breadcrumbs, a trickle of olive oil, then into a moderate oven for half an hour.

Roast Eel

Eels have become one of my firm favourites after a tremendous experience I had with them on the Po, the time I was filming *La Donna del Fiume* (*The Woman of the River*). Until then like many people I was inclined to fight shy of this huge serpentine creature. But one evening the whole troupe was invited to a dinner by the President of the Azienda Valley of Comacchio (the network of lakelike tributaries formed by the Po delta).

The dinner was held in a remote part of the countryside lost among the lakes and the canals, the only habitations being fishermen's huts. Rustic tables had been laid in the open, and set with whatever knives, forks, and plates could be scraped together for the occasion. It was a beautiful night, ten or fifteen gigantic bonfires blazed on river flats and reflected endlessly in the softly lapping waters of the lake – a dream atmosphere among those country folk who were so used to enormous silences and were now being so gay and sociable for one gala evening. They brought us seven great dishes of eel and if we hadn't been told beforehand what it was, we would never have guessed that in each of them was the same fish: eel cooked in seven different ways. The cooking of that white delicate flesh was so elaborate. (I remember one other curious detail. Our host, an ardent fancier of eel, surprised us by making a point of telling us that his greatest passion was – eel heads! and in each, stuffed with tiny, tiny pieces of the flesh, he found the most incomparable *recherché* flavours.)

As far as I am concerned the most perfect way of serving eel is simply to roast it on an open fire. But there are a few points to bear in mind.

First of all: you must skin the eel. Make a slit around the neck cutting through the skin, wrap the head in cloth, hold tight and peel the skin back toward the tail, freeing stubborn places with a knife. Now slit the eel open right down its belly to clean the intestine and remove the bone; dust it with salt, then cook it on the grill, giving it a turn from time to time. One last word of advice: never baste eels with oil. If you are cooking them this way, let them roast in their own fat.

Eel on the Spit

If the eel is fat enough you can roast it on the spit instead on the grill. In this case, after you have skinned it (as in the previous recipe) and slit open the belly just enough to remove the intestine etc., cut the eel into pieces 2 or 3 inches long, sprinkle with oil, salt, pepper, and thread the pieces on to the spit with bay leaves between each piece. Now you cook them on the open fire as you patiently turn your spit. One refinement, though: when the eel is practically cooked, sprinkle it with a finely chopped bay leaf mixed with breadcrumbs to form a sort of crust. When the eel is exactly cooked, it is nice and crunchy.

Stewed Eel

Skin and clean the eels in the usual way and cut them into pieces. Then fry a chopped onion and a spoonful of chopped parsley in 2 tablespoonfuls olive oil. A minute or two later you add the pieces of eel (1 pound of them) and wait a few minutes. Then toss about ¼ pint of dry white wine into the pan. When the wine is reduced, pour over a sauce you have prepared separately by sautéing 2 peeled, coarsely chopped tomatoes in 2 tablespoonfuls olive oil with a few minced basil leaves.

Let it cook until the pieces of eel are soft and the stew smoothly blended. Serve hot with little squares of oven-toasted bread. Enough for 2–4 persons.

Grilled Baccalà

Baccalà, as you may know, is salt cod, i.e. preserved in brine, and not to be confused with stockfish, which is cod dried in the sun and wind. In many regions of Italy – Venice, Naples, Rome, Tuscany, and so on – baccalà (and stockfish) is an extremely popular item on the menus in the small unpretentious *trattorias* and among the poor. It isn't hard to see why: it costs next to nothing and lends itself to the imagination of the poor (so often it is poverty which sparks off the brilliant ideas) who have turned it into a tasty and often absolutely delicious food. I've heard that in ages past the dried cod and the herring have saved the whole of Europe from catastrophic famines.

Now, to make grilled baccalà (and also for other ways as we shall see later) you must pay close attention to the following instructions: whenever possible buy the baccalà ready for cooking, because it has to be carefully prepared in order to soften it and draw off the excess of salt. Two pounds is enough for 6 persons. If you buy it softened and cut into pieces, there will be no further problem; but make very sure that it has stood long enough in water to be really suitable for cooking, and that the shopkeeper gives you the best parts, thick and soft, and not just the flat bony section near the tail. If you should have to buy the baccalà unprepared, you must keep it under cold running water for a day or two. (Twenty-four hours are almost enough, but the results are never as good.) To do this it must be placed in a basin under the tap with a continuous trickle of water. When it is soft, cut it into chunks, removing the bones; then drain these chunks thoroughly on a cloth until perfectly dry.

If you want to grill them as we used to do at home when I was a little girl, you simply put the chunks of baccalà (remember they must be cut thick) under the grill. It is even better if you have a grill over an open fire. Keep on turning them so that they cook consistently. When they are done, baste and season with a simple sauce of oil, finely chopped garlic, and rosemary.

Fried Baccalà

Prepare the baccalà and cut it as described in the previous recipe, but in much smaller pieces. Dust each piece in flour and fry in plenty of good olive oil. Serve with slices of lemon and sprigs of parsley.

Baccalà Salad

Prepare 2 pounds of baccalà as in the first recipe, but this time cut in larger pieces; stew in the minimum quantity of water, and add a tablespoonful of olive oil and a slice of lemon. At the same time you should boil a good-sized cauliflower in salted water. Then cut both the baccalà and cauliflower into dice and add to them about 3 ounces of stoned and chopped green olives, a handful of chopped parsley, as much olive oil as necessary to coat all lightly, a spoonful or two of vinegar, to taste, and a pinch of pepper.

Baccalà in Tomato Sauce

First fry the pieces of baccalà as for Fried Baccalà, then put them in a baking dish, and cover with a good tomato sauce to which you may add a few chopped, stoned olives and a handful of parsley. Put into a moderate oven (375°F.) for 15 minutes, and it is ready.

Livorno Baccala

This is another of my tasty short-cut versions of a famous recipe.

For 6 persons, soak 2 pounds of baccalà in the usual way, cut it into medium-sized pieces, put into a fireproof casserole with 2–3 tablespoonfuls of olive oil, a pound or more of tinned tomatoes, a pinch of oregano and a chopped garlic clove. Cook over a slow flame. When half cooked (after about 10 minutes), add a dozen or so stoned black olives, which will lend more tang.

Baccalà alla Vizcayna

When I was filming *El Cid* in Spain, as on other occasions, the *baccalà alla vizcayna* (which means it is cooked in the Bay of Biscay style) always reminded me of the baccalà we have at home in Italy. The main difference being the addition of pimientos; so I was eager to know how to make it.

Soak two pounds of baccalà as usual, cut into pieces, dry well, dust in flour and brown lightly in olive oil. Then take the pieces out of the pan and lay them on porous paper to soak out all the oil, but without letting them cool. Meanwhile, put 3 tablespoonfuls of olive oil in a pan and a couple of sliced onions; let the onion brown and reduce in the oil over a moderate flame. Then add 1 pint or slightly more of sieved tomato pulp; sprinkle with salt and pepper; let cook longer until a thick but still liquid sauce begins to form.

Cook separately 2–3 fresh pimientos (or 1 large sweet red pepper) in an unoiled pan over fairly high heat just until the skins shrivel; let cool, then very delicately tear the skins off, (if possible without wetting them, just dipping your fingertips in water from time to time). Take out the cores and the seed, and cut the flesh into pieces, then put them in the pan again with a drop of oil and sprinkling of salt. Final operation: put the pieces of fried baccalà into a baking pan, pour the pimientos over them, and then the sauce: place in a hot oven (425°F.) for about ten minutes or even less. It's ready.

DIGRESSION
(On Wines)

On Brioni, that enchanting Istrian island in the Adriatic, I have often been the guest of the President of Yugoslavia, Tito, whose friendship I am honoured to enjoy. Tito is the soul of affability, and, well over seventy, he still has a hearty love of good eating. At table he is a perfect host, kindly, amusing, and with a great appreciation of fine wine. At his luncheons a white local wine is served which is a joy, closely related to our light white wines of the Veneto. The first time I tasted this wine I immediately wanted to know where it came from. Tito, who was obviously delighted by my curiosity, pointed to a small (so to speak) vineyard through the window. The good President told me that every year he personally attended the harvest. In late summer every year he invites a great number of his ministers and friends and puts them all to work, under the orders of the expert peasant farmer. It is a gay and extraordinarily rapid harvest, which of course is exactly what Tito intends it to be. Picking and pressing and barrelling. There is no other intermediate operation. That is why the wine is the most natural, the most genuine you can imagine.

I have told you about Tito's vineyard in order to introduce my own dogma about wines. The guarantee of a good wine does not consist in the more or less famous trade marks on the bottles but in the confidence one has in its genuineness. A modest wine but one which you can say that you are absolutely sure is genuine is worth much more than a famous wine which you haven't seen grow, so to speak, before your eyes. In my country villa in Marino in the Roman hills (an area famous for its wines, the so-called *vini dei Castelli*), we make several barrels of white wine every year. And not a single guest who dines at our villa but asks for it, forgetting all the renowned wines of

Europe which might equally well be demanded from our cellar.

However, genuineness apart and taken for granted, a good wine is very important, even essential for proper dining. This knowledge, however, must be a joy and not allowed to become an excessive complication. I mean that certain basic rules are enough to resolve all drink problems at lunch or dinner. And I get very fed up with people who show off the wine culture which they don't really possess and which boils down to a sadly transformed self-glorification, or, as they say in France, *pour épater le bourgeois.*

For me, a real expert is always a fascinating person and one of them is my dear friend, Robert Favre Le Bret, for many years Director of the Cannes Film Festival. And it was with him that I met one of these so-called connoisseurs. We were together at a dinner party among friends and one of them kept on at the sommelier, an elderly and most reputable gentleman, talking six to the dozen about vintage years, labels, *châteaux, crus,* the character of a wine, and so on, and manged to get on everyone's nerves. I glanced at Favre Le Bret, who could have withered him with one word. But, generously, Favre Le Bret did not open his mouth.

So what can I possibly have to say on the same subject? This is a book about my own cookery and not a treatise on cooking. And I can't claim to be able to discuss wine like a real connoisseur. So I shall simply tell you what I know.

First of all, in Italy you can't conceive of a proper dinner without wine. Milk, tea, fruit juice, of course, are wonderful drinks, but with a plate of spaghetti or a dish of fried fish, or roast lamb, I don't honestly think that there can be any doubt. You need wine. There is really a constant tie-up between food and wine which follows on from course to course. And this is the test of a real gourmet. He conceives a dinner, not on a collection of dishes but as a sequence of dishes with the right wines.

If we are agreed so far, there are other things to bear in mind. You must maintain a certain order in serving wine and you must serve it carefully. To start with, as everyone knows, white should always precede red. White goes very well with antipasti (champagne too), and with soup and fish. The more cheerful younger reds go well with certain soups (but then the menu must be so arranged that no further white wine is necessary). The more full-bodied reds go with meat dishes. The most noble reds are usually reserved for roasts or game. With sweets come the heavier sweet wines like port, marsala, muscat, and the like.

This sequence of wines is, of course, a question of taste. Changing the wine does no serious harm – contrary to what many people believe. If one follows the right sequence, from the white to the red, from the lighter to the heavier. What does do harm is to get the sequence wrong. And then nobody can prevent you from drinking just one wine at table, a wine which is not too strong, but light and cheerful, which goes with everything. The ideal – well-known but rather expensive – is, of course, to accompany your food exclusively with champagne.

The art of composing the perfect menu is an art which is acquired with patience and close attention. I don't claim to be able to outline it here but I would like to add a few words on how to store and serve wine.

First of all, remember that wine closed in the bottle and protected by the cork leads a slow life, like a fakir buried alive. It is a sort of lethargy which must never be disturbed. So keep it in a dark place where the temperature is as constant as you can make it, where it will meet with the minimum possible vibration, or smells, which could penetrate the cork and spoil the taste.

For the same reason, a bottle, especially if it is a very old one, must be handled and carried with great care to the table. Before opening it, it must have reached the right temperature which for a full-bodied red must be 64°F. For other reds it is

61°F. and even less for the light, unpretentious whites, which are pleasant only if they give a sense of freshness. A wine connoisseur would shudder at this last statement, but I am not speaking of *noble* wines just now: in these matters you want a certain elasticity according to the season. But don't, whatever you do, over-chill white wines. A good white should remain at 46°F. or 48°F. even more; others are served lower. Champagne itself should never be drunk iced. It loses its taste and upsets the stomach. For a connoisseur, the temperature should never fall lower than 39°F.

It is important to know exactly when to open the bottle. Remember, the moment the wine comes in contact with the air, it rouses from its lethargy and lives at a livelier rhythm: in this way it reacquires all its splendour. So a bottle of old, generous red will improve if you open it a few hours before drinking. You can even open it the day before. The white take less time, an hour or so.

When you give a dinner party, go to great trouble with these details, whether at home or not. In the last phase, when you pour the wine into the glass, you must do it very gently, as wine is a delicate thing.

If you feel you would like to follow these tips of mine at your next dinner party, then there is one thing only I ask: that you drink to my health as well.

Meat

These are the meat recipes from my repertoire, including those for liver, tripe, etc. They do not include poultry and game, which, as in all cookery books, have a chapter to themselves, owing to the fundamental differences in preparation. The recipes that follow are mostly for meat dishes and stews and casseroles from my own kitchen or those I have discovered on my travels in different countries of the world. At this point I would like to make it quite clear that when I speak of a meat sauce or ragout, be it Neapolitan or Genoese, at the beginning of this chapter, I am not repeating the recipe for Ragout given in the section on home-made pasta, Fettuccine. There is a difference. Ragout for pasta contains minced meat mixed with other ingredients; while a meat ragout is a dish in itself with *involtini* and chunks of meat meant to be sliced, even though the sauce which results may do very well as a dressing for pastasciutta.

Neapolitan Meat Ragout

You need 6 slices of beef, one for each person, preferably cut from the *noce* (sirloin tip), and 4–5 ounces each. Pound them, cut away the gristle, then on each slice spread a spoonful of a mixture made of 2 good handfuls of chopped parsley, 2 or 3 minced garlic cloves, a good pinch each of pepper and salt. Roll up the slices (involtini), and spear them with a wooden toothpick, then lay them in a saucepan in a little olive oil over a fierce flame. As soon as the outside of the meat begins to brown, pour over the meat about ¼ pint of dry white wine and then lower the flame; then, when the wine is completely consumed, pour in 3 pounds of peeled, coarsely chopped tomatoes. From now on you simply cook the meat over a slow heat, for a minimum of an hour and a half. When it is done, you can eat the involtini and use the sauce for any kind of pasta.

Genoese Meat Ragout

It is odd that this ragout, which tastes so different from the one in the last recipe because it contains onion instead of tomato, should be called Genoese, because it is even more Neapolitan than the other. Friends who are experts in these matters have explained that it is an original recipe used in Neapolitan households before the discovery of America, when the tomato was still unknown. But why it should be known as Genoese nobody can say. In honour of Christopher Columbus? I hardly think so, because part of Columbus's business in opening the new world was to become the pioneer of the tomato, which is just the thing the Genoese ragout so proudly turns its back on. Whatever the answer, here is how to make it:

You need 6 slices of sirloin tip, each weighing 4–5 ounces, one for each person. Pound and trim as for Neapolitan Meat Ragout. On each slice, however, you put about 1½ teaspoonfuls of grated Parmesan, a pinch of chopped parsley, a piece of carrot and pepper and salt. Roll them up to form the involtini and tie with white thread or secure with wooden toothpicks.

Meanwhile, heat a pan with 4–5 tablespoonfuls of olive oil, and 2 pounds of thinly sliced onions. When the onions begin to blanch, place the involtini in the pan beside them, cover and let them cook for a few hours until the meat has become extremely tender and the onions have melted into a thick sauce blending with the juice from the meat. This is the classic, authentic Genoese recipe, where not only the tomatoes are missing but also the wine. You can let the juice concentrate until it becomes a real sauce to be poured over the meat in the serving dish; but the custom is to take it off at a more liquid stage and use it on pastasciutta. To be perfectly honest I must admit that these days many Neapolitan women are inclined to put a little tomato purée into the pot to heighten the colour.

Involtini

This recipe follows the previous ones, but it has one special feature: the involtini are real involtini, that is they are much smaller and the filling is more carefully made so that there is more flavour. The sauce isn't so important.

You need, then, for 6 people, 12 thin slices of lean beef (fillet or sirloin tip), each about 2½ ounces at the most. Give them a light pounding and cover each with a slice of Bologna mortadella; roll and spear them together with wooden toothpicks. Brown them in a pan with olive oil in which you have previously and briefly browned a garlic clove. That is all for the moment. When the involtini have turned brown over a fairly fierce flame, toss about ¼ pint of dry white wine over them; then add lashings of tomatoes, 2 pounds even, salt and pepper, and a few young minced basil leaves. From now on the cooking should continue on a low heat for over an hour.

Braciole

My own name for these steaks is *involtoni* which means big involtini because they are also rolled slices of meat. The problem is that in the north of Italy braciole is the regular name for beefsteak. But as regards the recipe, it isn't simply a case of making your involtinis bigger. It is something quite different.

Start with 3 slices of fillet of beef, each weighing about 8 ounces – don't worry about the size because later each will be cut to serve 2 people – pound them, but not too hard, then cut away the fat and pieces of gristle and set aside while you make the following filling.

First of all chop together 1½ ounces of salt pork fat, a clove of garlic and a good handful of parsley. Then have ready some very thin slices of ham and 6 of Provolone cheese, also 2 spoonfuls of well-washed sultanas and another 2 of pine nuts. Now over each cut of meat lay a slice of ham and one of cheese; then a little of the pork fat chopped with parsley and garlic; then a few sultanas and pine nuts. Roll up the meat around the filling, tie it with a thick string, and cook it in a pan with a regular Neapolitan Meat Ragout. Bear in mind, though, that the cooking will take much longer, even a couple of hours. When you see that the braciole are properly cooked and the meat is quite tender, lift them out of the pan, and leave the juice to reduce into a good thick sauce. Then put the braciole back for a minute or two to heat and absorb more of the sauce. Don't forget that the braciole are the first to go into the serving dish, then a covering of the sauce.

Truffled Beef on Skewers

For this you need to marinate a good cut of beef (fillet or sirloin tip) for an hour or so in enough olive oil to cover it completely, plus the juice of a lemon, a teaspoonful of salt, a few peppercorns, a little chopped parsley and oregano. When the time comes to cook the meat, take it out of the oil, cut it into cubes and thread them on to skewers, with very thin slices of salt pork between each one. As you roast the skewered meat on the fire, baste from time to time with the marinade. When it is on the serving dish, cover with thin slivers of truffle. Out of all the variations you can play on the theme of skewered meat, this one is rhapsody.

Roast Beef

As soon as I had my first plate of roast beef in England, I noticed the difference at once. In France and in other countries roast beef is always supposed to be blood red; whereas in England the classical roast beef is a pale rose inside and brown on the outside. I asked how it was cooked (I always do whenever I enjoy a dish), and here is the formula they consider the best.

First you have to tie, bind, or skewer the rib or sirloin roast to keep it round and thick; use kidney fat for grease if possible (butter is a good substitute, but no more than a substitute); then roast on a spit, or at least on an open grill, never allowing the meat to come into contact with the bottom of the pan. Time of roasting depends on the weight and thickness of the meat, but by prodding the top of the beef from time to time, you have a pretty good idea of when it is ready. (Be very careful, however, not to make holes in the surface with a fork while it is cooking, otherwise you will lose the precious juices. Prod only when you are sure the beef is practically done.) Now all you have to do is carve. There are two schools of thought about carving: thick slices or thin? I go for a thick slice every time.

Boiled Meat

For those who like boiled meat I could write pages and pages. In Italy and especially in Piedmont, they serve a whole series of boiled meats; different cuts of beef including the tongue; calf's head; *cotechino* (a pigskin stuffed with chopped salt pork); a capon or a boiling hen. But nobody would dream of embarking on a dish like this without having a large crowd of people to sit down to it; a *bollito* is for a special occasion and needs a great deal of care and attention.

Personally I think one can make a very passable bollito with only two cuts of beef: rump and rib. The reason for these cuts is that rump is leaner and more compact while the rib beef is fatter, but of a tender fat which contrasts deliciously in taste with the lean. Both pieces must cook for a fairly long time for the beef to tenderize and cut easily, but they must not be overcooked otherwise they will lose their best juices and taste like stewed string. It seems to me the best system is to cook the two pieces, each weighing about 1 lb. 8 oz. if 6 people are to be served, in about 2½ quarts of water in a big pot. As soon as the water starts to boil, first skim off all the froth from the surface; then add a couple of whole peeled onions, each with a clove embedded, a couple of carrots or sticks of celery, a few small chopped tomatoes, peppercorns, and a good pinch of salt. Altogether the cooking should last for about 3 hours, with the heat turned down to the point where the water is just below boiling. When it is ready, the bollito is served hot, in a serving dish containing a few tablespoonfuls of stock to keep it moist. With it you can serve any variety of sharp sauces, or pickles or various vegetables. My favourite accompaniment is this one: over a good-sized slice of boiled beef pour a trickle of olive oil, a few lumps of coarse kitchen salt, and dust with freshly ground black pepper. Heaven!

Boiled Meat and Tomatoes

If you have any cold boiled beef left over, you can revive it into a delicious dish like this:

Cut off a slice about ¼-inch thick, then drop it into a pan in which you have already browned about 8 ounces of chopped onions in a few tablespoonfuls of olive oil. When the meat browns, sprinkle with pepper and salt, stir it around, then pour in a liberal dash of dry wine. Wait for the wine to reduce, then add a few large red tomatoes, finely sliced, and if necessary a few spoonfuls of stock or warm water. Let it cook a little longer then drop in a few very young leaves of basil.

Boiled Beef alla Pizzaiola

You can also revitalize left-overs of boiled beef this way: put some olive oil in a pan with a mixture of chopped garlic and parsley; add a pinch of oregano, and a large helping of very thinly sliced tomato. Then put in the beef, cut into slices. Wait for it to heat, sprinkle with salt and pepper, and as it cooks, add to the juices, if need be, a few spoonfuls of stock or warm water.

Beef Roasted in Salt

This isn't, of course, roast beef proper, but the same cut of beef you use for roasting. Get the butcher to give you a piece of rolled sirloin tip weighing 3 pounds at least for 6 people, and see that you have a good supply of coarse kitchen salt. Put down a layer of the salt one inch deep in the bottom of a roasting pan; place the meat on top; then go on adding the salt until the beef is entirely buried with about ½-inch of salt on top of it. Place in a moderate oven, and cook until the outer layer of salt has acquired a reddish tinge. Then cut away the salt crust, free the meat inside, and brush away (a small paint brush is invaluable in the kitchen) the last grains of salt from the roast (no kind of fat or oil in this recipe). Now you can serve it in slices and accompany with pickles or fried potatoes. You will have absolutely no need of any other sort of condiment. At the very most you might lay a sprig of rosemary on top of the meat under its casing of salt.

Steak and Onions

Any good-quality steak, about 2 inches thick, can be cooked this way. Instead of grilling it, you cook it in a pan (taking great care not to puncture it with a fork otherwise it will shed its juice and lose flavour). Before cooking the steak, however, you should have prepared some sliced onions, fried in a pan with olive oil and butter, salt, pepper, and a hearty pinch of sugar. When the onions blanch, put them aside somewhere where they will keep hot. Brown the steak in the pan and when it is ready, pour the onions on top, stir for a moment, then serve.

Steak with Mushrooms

Cooked the same way as Steak and Onions, but this time you finish up by smothering the steak with mushrooms instead of onions. First you slice the mushrooms, very thin if they are fresh, or in chunks if dried (naturally you must first of all revive the dried mushrooms by soaking them in warm water), and sauté in a little butter. Season with a small pinch of salt and, at the very end, a good pinch of chopped parsley.

Steak with Caper Sauce

This time you prepare a caper sauce instead of onions or mushrooms for your steak. A few spoonfuls of olive oil in a small pan, and for each steak you put in a handful of chopped capers and a minced anchovy fillet. Wait for the anchovy to run and the sauce to bind before you cook your steaks. Then cover with the sauce. NOTE: Don't salt the steaks – the sauce is salty enough.

Barbecue Sauces

Although very much an American speciality, in Europe we, too, bestow on barbecues the appreciation they deserve. I can remember one marvellous one at the Burgenstock Golf Club in Switzerland where I sometimes go on holidays. The great novelty here was that the meat was roasted on a fire made from branches of grapevine, which gave it an extraordinary, unforgettable bouquet. They tell me that in Sardinia they roast pork, boar, and whole lambs in the open, with the aromatic wood from the forests near the seashore. I have a passion for this sort of thing. And so very humbly may I suggest one or two sauces which are not so well known, and which you can spread over your roast meat to give it that final exquisite touch?

PEVERADA SAUCE

This is an ancient Venetian sauce used for roast guinea fowl, but it goes very well with other meat, in my opinion. Chop up and mix into paste the following ingredients: 7 ounces of calf's liver, a couple of anchovy fillets, a couple of garlic cloves, the peel of a lemon (first cutting off the white pith); a few onions, 2 or 3 pickled chilipeppers, a good pinch of pepper, 2 tablespoonfuls of grated Parmesan and 2 tablespoonfuls of breadcrumbs. Mix all these into a smooth paste and put aside.

Now heat in a pan two tablespoonfuls of olive oil and a whole clove of garlic. When the garlic blanches, take it out of the pan and add the paste, let it frizzle a little, adding drop by drop 2 or 3 teaspoonfuls of vinegar and ⅛ teaspoonful of ginger. You should make the sauce thick or thin according to whether you want to spread it on the pieces of meat, or serve it separately to dip the meat into on your plate.

ROQUEFORT SAUCE

Mix 4 ounces of Roquefort cheese with 2 to 3 ounces of butter and about the same amount of whipped cream. When they are smoothly blended, beat into them, with a wooden spoon, the juice of 2 shallots or 2 small onions and a teaspoonful of Worcestershire Sauce (or 2, if you want the flavour sharper). When the paste has become perfectly smooth, use it to dress beefsteaks and other roast meat.

Châteaubriand

For a Châteaubriand it is essential to have the right cut of meat, the piece which comes from the centre of the entire fillet of beef; and even if it is very big (otherwise it would not be a true Châteaubriand) it will still serve only 2 or 3 people. Grill it in the simplest way possible: first on one side, then on the other; just enough to cook without losing its tenderness. A sprinkling of salt and pepper at the very end.

Marinated Châteaubriand

This variation is one of the greatest eating pleasures I have ever encountered. And it never fails to remind me that Paris is a paradise of good cooking.

First let the Châteaubriand marinate for a whole day in 2 or 3 tablespoonfuls of olive oil mixed with a chopped or crushed garlic clove, a tablespoonful of vinegar, a sprig of rosemary, a pinch of pepper and one of salt. Just brush the mixture on the steak; you should turn it over at intervals. When the time for cooking comes, drain the steak thoroughly of excess marinade; grill it normally without even a hint of more pepper or salt.

Cotoletta alla Milanese

All the chefs in Milan are understandably proud of this *cotoletta;* they all are ready, with the best of arguments, to prove that Wienerschnitzel is no more than a derivation, and *not* vice versa. It is in fact a veal cutlet which can weigh anything up to 7 or 8 ounces (*cotoletta* is dialect Italian for the word for cutlet *costoletta*). It is dipped in oil and breadcrumbs and browned in butter. But there is more to it than that, if you go in at all for perfection.

First of all, the cutlet must have a handle, i.e. the bone attached, so order veal rib or loin chops. When served, this bone must be covered with a pretty little cap of paper, cut out like a daisy. Quite apart from appearances, I always find that cooking with the bone and the fatty part underneath gives a tremendous lift to the flavour. Then, too, you must see that the veal is thick enough without being too thick; roughly a shade under ½ inch. When it comes to the cooking, the simplest way is to dip the chop in beaten egg yolk, then in breadcrumbs and to fry it in melted butter. But it is even nicer (a little heavier, too!) if you prepare it the old-fashioned way: first a very quick dip in melted butter, then into the breadcrumbs, then the egg, then into the breadcrumbs again, then a browning in melted butter. The crust will be a joy in itself.

Sophia as she might look in a portrait entitled: Woman with Fruit (Photo Secchiaroli)

Chicken cooked on an original spit which Sophia has had installed by the Marino swimming pool (Photo Soldati)

Sophia adds the finishing touch to one of her ice cream desserts (Photo Soldati)

The kitchen of a famous restaurant in Emilia, where Sophia has seen many of her recipes made (Photo Secchiaroli)

Bolognese Cutlet

This is the pride of the chefs of Bologna, who have every reason to claim their city as the capital of the Italian *cucina* like Lyons in France.

You take slices of veal but not necessarily chops this time, weighing about 4 ounces each. Flatten them a little, but not too much – they should be just under a ½ inch thick. Then dip in egg yolk and breadcrumbs, brown in lard or, failing lard, butter. Until now we have followed in the footsteps of Cotoletta alla Milanese; but there is more to come. Now, you lay over the crumbled cutlet a slice of ham, a handful of grated Parmesan and a few slivers of truffle. Now that they are properly dressed your cutlets may enter the baking dish packed fairly tightly. Place in a hot oven (425°F.) just long enough for the cheese to melt and bind the truffle and ham to the meat.

Stracotto with Mushrooms

The first step is to marinate a good-sized piece of beef rump roast or sirloin tip (3–4 pounds for 6–8 people) for several hours, usually overnight. You make the marinade, allowing about ⅓ pint of dry red wine for every pound of meat; then throw in a sliced onion and a chopped stick of celery, a couple of crushed garlic cloves, peppercorns, and only one or two bay leaves. Before entering the marinade the meat should be wrapped or draped with strips of bacon.

When the time comes for cooking, put a thinly sliced onion into a pan with about 4 ounces chopped ham fat; as the onion glazes, add the piece of meat, which you have removed from the marinade, dried off with a cloth and then dipped in flour. Wait until the meat is browned on all sides (you must keep turning it), then add 4 ounces sliced mushrooms. Immediately afterwards, add the marinade itself to the pan, sprinkle in salt, and let the meat cook long and slowly without using a lid, now and then checking to see that the bottom of the pan hasn't dried up (if it has, spoon in a little stock or warm water). And that is all. It will take about 3 hours. Slice the meat and cover it with the sauce which has been taken from the pan and put through a sieve.

Stew Italian Style

Here is a very historic recipe for cooking beef. This time, instead of marinating the meat, put a rump or sirloin tip roast straight into the pot. For every 2 pounds of beef (allow 1 pound for every 2 persons) you will want 6 tablespoonfuls of olive oil, a tablespoonful of butter, then enough onion, celery, carrots, potatoes, turnips, all cut up into small chunks, to cover the meat. Start cooking on a fierce flame; when all is hot, turn heat to low and add a sprinkling of pepper and salt; put the lid on and leave pot on a very low heat. It will take anything from 2 to 3 hours before the meat is completely cooked. Slice the beef, run the sauce through a sieve and pour it over the meat at the last moment. The addition of a trickle of olive oil and the juice of one lemon will do wonders for the taste.

Spezzatino or Italian Goulash

This is the Italian version of Hungarian goulash. The best meat for this is shin beef, because as the gristle and tendons soften in the cooking, they become permeated with delicious flavours which are much appreciated by the gourmets. Some people may prefer to make spezzatino with leaner, more compact chunks of meat, but they are making a big mistake. Because if it isn't made the proper way, spezzatino can be a very dreary dish. So ask your butcher to give you shin beef already cut into pieces, about 3 pounds for 6 people, and set to work.

Begin cooking 3–4 tablespoonfuls of minced pork fat (failing that: olive oil or butter) with a tablespoonful of chopped onion and a minced garlic clove, a few leaves of marjoram, and a stick of celery. As soon as they begin to change colour, add the meat and sprinkle with pepper and salt. As it starts to brown, drench with about ½ pint of dry white wine; let the wine reduce, and then pour in ¼ pint of good tomato sauce, and finally ¾ to 1 pint of stock or warm water to prevent the pan from drying out. Cover and leave it bubbling on a very low heat. It should take a couple of hours, but check often and add a little extra stock if the pan threatens to dry out. At this point add slices of boiled potato and cook them together for a few minutes so that they absorb the sauce. Serve.

Polpette
(Meat Balls)

Mix minced beef, grated Parmesan cheese, eggs, and breadcrumbs into a consistent paste. Shape your meat balls from the mixture and fry them in a pan with oil and butter, and if you feel like adding tomato and various herbs so much the better. But everyone who cooks or loves good cooking will have his own formula, so a meat ball mixture will always have a personal touch about it and some special ingredient. The recipe I would like to suggest was taught to me by a friend in Milan.

You start off by mincing two parts of beef with one of chicken (1 pound and 8 ounces, say). Add a few pieces of sausage or salami (but not more than 1½ ounces); bind with 2 eggs, 2 tablespoonfuls of breadcrumbs (3 if the paste gets too sticky); the same of grated Parmesan, a pinch of salt, one of pepper and one of nutmeg. Shape your meat balls rather small and put them in a pan with only a little olive oil. When they are frying, lift the pan from the stove and pour off some of the oil, leaving only a film at the bottom. Then return to the heat and add 1½ pints of thin cream and 2 or 3 tablespoonfuls of ketchup, then cook for another 10 minutes so that the meat balls get softer and the sauce thickens.

Oriental Meat Loaf

I used to adore this when I was on the Red Sea, but you don't necessarily have to be in the Middle East to make it. For 6 persons, shape 2 lb. 8 oz. – 3 lb. beef into a squat round; sprinkle it with pepper and salt, very finely chopped garlic (or better still, crushed), and cumin seeds. Make a cavity in the centre of the meat and insert two hard-boiled eggs (shelled, naturally!). Now roll the meat round the eggs to form a meat loaf, paint it with beaten egg yolk, dip it in breadcrumbs, and then place it in a pan with 3–4 tablespoonfuls of olive oil. When the loaf begins to brown on the outside, pour into the pan enough tomato sauce almost to cover and add a pinch of salt. Finish cooking without further ado. The loaf is served sliced in its own sauce. The two hard-boiled eggs are really there to stop the centre from emerging uncooked, but they are also very good with the meat.

Roast Veal

Buy a good-sized veal shoulder or rump (3–5 pounds). Then it must be tied with string or secured with skewers before putting into the oven so that it will keep its shape and remain compact. Sprinkle it with salt and place it in a large baking pan with about 2–3 ounces each of olive oil and lard (or just the oil if lard isn't available). Slice into the dish about 8 ounces each of onions and tomatoes. Roast in a hot oven, basting frequently with dripping, about 1½–2 hours. Then cut into slices and serve surrounded with the tomatoes and onions.

Veal alla Pizzaiola

Have some veal fillet cut into thin slices weighing about 1½ ounces each. You'll need about 2 pounds for 6 persons. Pound them lightly, then brown quickly in 3–4 tablespoonfuls of olive oil. Add 2 peeled and cut up tomatoes, a minced garlic clove, oregano, salt and pepper to taste. Let cook slowly about 10 minutes, then add a good splashing of dry white wine (about ¼ pint). Let cook a few minutes more until sauce reduces slightly, then serve.

Piccatine of Veal

These should be thin little slices of veal fillet, no more than 1 ounce each. Allow about 2 pounds for 6 people. A brisk sprinkling of salt, then dip veal into flour and brown in butter for a few minutes. They will already be very tasty, but you usually finish them off with a little sauce made from diced raw ham (about 4–6 ounces) frizzled in the butter left in the pan. When the ham has lost its raw look, squeeze into the pan the juice of a quarter of a lemon. Then pour the sauce over the slices of veal, scatter a little chopped parsley on top, and your *piccatine* are ready for the table.

Saltimbocca alla Romana

The name alone is enough to make one's mouth water, the mere idea of these delicate little squares of meat, so exquisite that they leap (*saltare*) straight into your mouth (*bocca*) of their own accord.

To make them you need small, thin slices of veal round, the kind used for Piccatine, but maybe cut a shade thicker. For 6 people you will need about 2 pounds. Each slice is dusted with a little salt and pepper, then covered with a tissue-thin slice of ham (with a little fat on it to moisten the veal during the cooking). Then put one small sage leaf on each piece of ham. Now you roll up the saltimbocca (really a sort of glorified involtino) and spear with wooden toothpicks, then dip into a plate of flour. Melt 3–4 tablespoonfuls butter in a pan and cook the saltimbocca, turning them over so that all sides are browned. Then transfer them to a serving dish. To the butter and meat juices left in the pan, add ¼ pint of dry white wine, 1½ teaspoonfuls of flour and a little more pepper, wait for the wine to reduce before pouring the sauce over the saltimboccas.

Veal Escalopes

Again you need thin slices of veal fillet, but cut longer than for Piccatine and Saltimbocca. (Each should weigh a good 3–4 ounces.) Pound slices to flatten them (but not too heavily), sprinkle with salt and pepper, dip in a plate of beaten egg, then into flour and brown lightly in butter. *Ecco!*

Vitello Tonnato
(Veal with Tuna Fish Sauce)

Another Milanese speciality. It is made with plain cold roast veal cut into slices and covered with a creamy piquant sauce of tuna fish, anchovies, and capers. But the original recipe as I learned it goes rather differently.

To make a good Vitello Tonnato, you should set a leg of veal to marinate in dry white wine overnight (at least). For each 2 pounds of leg of veal, use ¾–1 pint of dry white wine; then add to the marinade a large chopped onion and a diced carrot, a couple of bruised garlic cloves, and pepper and salt. When properly marinated, the leg of veal is placed in a large stew pot with a little oil warmed over high heat. As soon as the veal blanches, pour in the marinade as well, cover, and let it cook slowly for about an hour. Once cooked, leave the veal to cool in its marinade, then cut into thin slices.

Sieve what remains in the pan with about 4–5 ounces of tuna fish, 3–4 anchovy fillets that have been rinsed free of salt and mashed, the yolks of 2 hard-boiled eggs, the juice of a lemon, 2 tablespoonfuls of olive oil, 1 of vinegar, and a pinch of sugar. Beat them up well into a thick sauce which you then use to cover the slices of veal. Garnish by scattering a few little capers over the top.

Pork Pot Roast

For this you need a pork shoulder roast weighing at least 3 pounds, which will serve 4–6 people. Pierce the meat all over with whatever you have in the kitchen drawer to make holes with, and fill the holes with a mixture of chopped parsley and garlic, pepper and salt. Then tie up the meat like a parcel so that it is compact and place it in a large saucepan with about 4 tablespoonfuls of olive oil. As the roast begins to brown, douse it with about ¾ pint of dry white wine. When the wine is reduced, pour a good 2 pounds of peeled, coarsely chopped fresh tomatoes, or 1½–2 pints of tinned tomatoes, into the pan, then cover and let cook over a slow fire for a couple of hours. When the meat is done, cut it into slices, arrange on a serving dish, and cover with the sauce that remains in the pan. Serve hot.

Porchetta
(Sucking Pig)

This is one of the great Roman dishes; in fact porchetta is what sucking pigs are called in Roman, i.e. a feminine form, instead of the masculine *maialino* which is the word in correct Italian. Usually the animal is a little older than a real sucking pig, 6 months being the best for slaughtering, so that the meat is tender without being too fat. You should make sure that all the blood is drained during the slaughtering. Moreover the skin should be scrupulously clean. Plunge the carcass into boiling water if necessary to eliminate bristles. You can of course buy raw sucking pigs ready prepared; but you should make sure the butcher hands over the heart and kidneys as well. When the time comes, clean and chop the offal, then fry it in salt pork fat, adding ¼ pint of dry white wine when the fat begins to brown. Keep it hot. Then brush the inside of the pig with lard, sprinkle with pepper and salt, then stuff it with the fried liver, heart, and kidneys; finally put in an abundant handful of rosemary. Close up the inside, and lard the outer skin, sprinkling with more salt; place in a large roasting pan and set in a very hot oven (475°F.). After about 10 minutes, reduce oven heat to moderate (375°F.) and continue to roast, allowing about 25 minutes per pound. The pig will soon start to exude juices, which you can then baste over it. One of the beauties of porchetta, which you eat in very thick slices, is that it is also delicious when it is cold – and therefore excellent party fare.

Cotechino *in Camicia*

This ancient Emilian recipe suddenly rocketed to fame in Italy when my friend and adviser Vincenzo Buonassisi gave it in his columns and over television. I have attempted to make it myself, and hope I have done due justice to his instructions; it is certainly a fantastic dish.

Your first operation is to plunge a cotechino (the large, soft, salt pork sausage from Emilia) in hot water in order to strip off its skin. Then it must go into its 'shirt' which is a broad, flat slice of veal (round is best). The veal must be sliced large enough to wrap around the cotechino; it must also be spread first with very finely chopped mushrooms. Roll the whole thing up and tie with string to prevent the 'shirt' from coming apart. Put in a large saucepan with about 5 tablespoonfuls olive oil, a stick of celery, an onion, 1 or 2 carrots, all cut into small chunks. You won't need salt and pepper because there is already enough in the cotechino. When the veal begins to brown, add warm water to the bottom of the saucepan (perhaps a pint), cover, and cook very slowly until the meat is done, in about 2 hours. To serve, you slice straight through the roll so that you have rings of veal meat surrounding the pink cotechino. The pieces of mushroom have of course become almost invisible during the cooking, but they give the meat the most beautiful flavour. You may then strain what remains in the pan and pour it over the slices of cotechino. If you happen to have added diced ham or bacon as well as vegetables, save what stays behind in the sieve. It will make an excellent dressing for tagliatelle.

Zampone and Lentils

This is the dish that graces every Italian dinner table on New Year's Day. It is said to bring luck. (This year the greatest happiness it brought to me was being able to spoon one or two mashed lentils into the mouth of my little Carlo.)

The first thing about *zampone* (cotechino meat stuffed

into a large pig's trotter and available in Italian delicatessens) is that it should be of good quality; for 6 people, you will need a 2-pound zampone. Before being cooked, the zampone must spend the night in a bath of cold water. When the time comes for cooking, prick the skin in several places with the biggest needle you have to keep it from splitting under the pressure of heat; then wrap the zampone very tightly in cheesecloth and tie round with string. Now you boil it in a very big saucepan in a great quantity of water. It will take 6 hours before it is properly done: the skin must be tender and the meat inside so soft that it almost melts in your mouth without losing its slightly aggressive flavour.

Cook the lentils according to the recipe for Pasta and Lentils in the Soups chapter. To serve, unwrap the zampone, cut in thick slices, and serve in a deep platter with the lentils.

Lamb and Peas

This is usually made from the breast or rib of lamb cut into chunks as for stew, but some people use veal instead. In either case, brown the pieces of meat in a pan in oil and butter (about 2 tablespoonfuls of each for 2 pounds of meat, which should serve 4 amply). When the meat has browned, add a chopped onion and a few parsley sprigs and let cook until the onion turns golden. Now add salt and pepper to season and about 1 pint of meat stock or water, cover and let cook slowly about 1–1½ hours until the meat is tender. About 15 minutes before serving, add a pound of shelled green peas, also adding, if necessary, a little more stock or water to keep the pan from cooking dry. When peas are done, serve.

VARIATIONS: Instead of peas you may add sliced artichokes or potatoes. Or artichokes and peas together. Here is one very savoury variation with lamb: when the meat is practically cooked, beat up two egg yolks with the juice of half a lemon, and pour in the pan away from the heat. The heat given off by the lamb will be sufficient to thicken the egg. Stir it once or twice, then serve.

Roast Lamb with Peas in Egg Sauce

This is one of my specialities, though I wouldn't claim it is my own invention. Actually there are two distinct operations. First you must roast a good leg of baby lamb weighing 3 pounds. Put it in a baking pan well greased with olive oil, with a sprig of rosemary and a few pieces of garlic. Pour over a little more olive oil, sprinkle with salt and pepper and place in a hot oven (425°F.) for about an hour and a half. When it is half done, baste with dry white wine and turn the leg so that it is well done on all sides.

Meanwhile fry a chopped onion with about 3 ounces of minced ham; add 1 lb. 4 oz. of shelled, small young green peas, cover and let them cook, adding, if necessary, a few tablespoonfuls of water to keep them moist. Beat up two eggs in a soup plate with two tablespoonfuls of grated Parmesan and a pinch of salt. As soon as the peas are cooked, pour them into a frying pan, iron if possible, together with the egg over a very hot flame. You haven't much time, so keep stirring briskly, otherwise you will be left with an omelette on your hands instead. The peas should just keep separated from the particles of egg. And that is all. Lay the roast lamb on the serving plate and surround it with the egg and peas. Serve instantly.

Moussaka

Here is another Oriental dish which in my opinion wins honours in any hemisphere. In 2 tablespoonfuls of olive oil fry half an onion, thinly sliced, and a minutely chopped clove of garlic; add a pound of mutton or lamb, cut into very small pieces (but not minced); continue with the cooking, stirring from time to time until a good rich sauce has formed. Into this slice 8 ounces of mushrooms and 8 ounces of coarsely chopped seeded tomatoes, then 2 tablespoons of tomato purée, a handful of chopped parsley, a small pinch of salt and one of ginger (or chili powder). It takes only a few minutes for everything to blend and the meat to cook. But don't allow it to get cold.

Now, without removing the skins, cut 5 or 6 aubergines into very thin slices, lengthwise, dip them in flour and drop them into hot olive oil. When they are lightly browned lay them on porous paper to drain off the oil.

We are nearly through. Grease a baking dish with only a little olive oil and fill it with a layer of aubergine, then a layer of meat, then another layer of aubergine, one of meat and a final layer of aubergine. Over the top sprinkle breadcrumbs and a trickle of oil. Then put the baking dish into a medium oven for 45 minutes–1 hour until a nice brown crust forms over your moussaka.

VARIATION: Some people put potatoes in their moussaka. In this case, start off with a layer of very thinly sliced potatoes in the baking dish and end with another layer on top. I would almost be inclined to say the potato version is the nicer. But you must have the oven hotter and leave the moussaka in longer for the thin slices of potato to be properly cooked.

ANOTHER VARIATION: Before placing the baking dish in the oven, pour in enough milk to cover everything. Then cook until the heat of the oven dries out all the milk and the moussaka is ready.

Méchoui

Méchoui is roast mutton as the Arabs do it. For me it always brings back the memory of a fabulous evening when I was making a film in the Sahara with John Wayne. A very important sheikh had invited us to dinner one night when shooting was almost over. He received us in his tent, as a brilliant moon reflected a fantastic light. We sat in the tent, on carpets worthy of a thousand and one nights. The canvas side-flaps were raised against a background of stars, as the spits revolved with their fragrant burdens. The mutton was served whole on a huge tray, and we had no problem about serving and eating with our fingers because the meat was so tender that it almost fell away from the bone. Our only worry was to avoid burning our fingers.

The whole secret, as they explained to me later, was cooking with enormous patience. If you can cook outdoors and you would like to try méchoui, here is the procedure. The mutton must be whole, as I said, completely skinned, and empty inside. Pass the skewer through it from head to tail. To hold it firm in the best position for cooking, tie the shoulders where they join the neck, and stretch the hind legs as horizontal as possible so that the whole carcass receives uniform heat from the coals. The spit should be standing about one foot above the fire. Then you begin to turn the beast for hours, without stopping.

I am sure the Arabs put their own aromatic herbs on the wood fire, but they are probably impossible to find anywhere in the West. The meat is seasoned only with rock salt and covered with melted salted butter. They explained to me that no other seasoning was needed because the meat of Arab mutton is already seasoned by the herbs of the local grazing ground, where wild thyme and others grow in abundance. And since you cannot really expect to find a Sahara sheep overnight, unless you have a magic lamp, you can at least make up for it by adding thyme leaves and other herbs both to the fire and to the inside of the carcass. In any case the meat is done when a fragrant golden crust forms over the outside of the beast.

If you like strong sensations, dip each mouthful in a curry sauce.

Liver alla Veneziana

My first suggestion is to clean the calf's liver by removing the membrane enclosing it (more to do but well worth the trouble) before you cut it into slices about ¼-inch thick (allow about 4–6 ounces per person). Begin the cooking by frying a quantity of sliced onions (2 onions for every pound of liver) and a few bay leaves in olive oil and butter (about 2 tablespoonfuls of each for 1 pound of liver). When the onions begin to blanch, but still haven't browned, take the pan from the heat and – second tip – only then add the slices of liver. Being very delicate, liver would harden immediately on sudden contact with strong heat. Over the liver sprinkle chopped parsley, salt and pepper, then put the pan back on the fire for about 10 minutes. Toward the end of the cooking, try to remove the bay leaves, toss in a little dry white wine (about a wineglass for each pound of liver) and wait for it to reduce. Serve.

Busecca alla Milanese
(Tripe alla Milanese)

There are lots of ways of cooking tripe in Italy. But for me the best is the way they do it in Milan, where it is known as *busecca* (which is why you sometimes hear the Milanese jokingly called *busecconi*).

For 4 persons, buy 2 pounds of clean washed tripe and boil it in a big pot of hot water, but only for a minute; then drain it carefully and cut it into strips the size of tagliatelle. This is the preparatory stage. Now heat 3 tablespoonfuls of butter with 3 tablespoonfuls of olive oil and slice in an onion. Add the busecca, then 8 ounces of large white dried beans (previously soaked, of course), and ½ pint of peeled and seeded tomatoes cut into pieces, a good spoonful of chopped celery, a pound of chopped carrots, a sprinkling of pepper and salt, a pinch of nutmeg and a few leaves of sage; then add stock (or warm water) until the whole is covered. Put a lid on the pot and let cook over a moderate heat for about 2 hours until very tender. These tripe tagliatelle are then dished out and dressed with grated Parmesan just like real tagliatelle or spaghetti.

Kidneys and Bacon

For 6 persons, buy smallish veal kidneys, say one for each 2 people, and soak them for half an hour in water with a good splash of vinegar in it. Meanwhile, heat 1 tablespoonful of butter, a sliced onion, a diced carrot and a scant 8 ounces of diced bacon in a pan. Cook over a moderate flame until the bacon takes on the flavour of the other ingredients without drying up (if necessary, moisten with a spoonful or two of stock).

Now for the kidneys. Take them out of the water, dry them, pull off the outer membrane, dip them lightly in flour, and cook them for about 5 minutes in several tablespoonfuls of butter in another pan over a high flame. Then cut them in half to remove the spongy gristle in the middle which has a nasty taste (this is an important tip which people often overlook). At this point, you can replace the kidneys in their pan, either the halves, or if kidneys are large, cut into thick slices: the main thing is not to lose the pink liquid which will run out as you cut them and gather at the bottom of the plate. Pour the liquid into the pan as well and continue with the cooking, now adding the fry of onions and bacon, a pinch of pepper and salt and about a wineglass of marsala. When the marsala is reduced, add a good handful of chopped parsley and immediately transfer the kidneys to the serving dish to be covered with the sauce which has now collected in the bottom of the pan. Serve.

Kidney alla Carnacina

This is another way of doing kidneys which I stole from Luigi Carnacina, undisputed king of Italian cooking, and famous throughout Europe and the rest of the world. His books have been translated into most foreign languages and are especially successful in the United States. Today Carnacina is over eighty, but I'm told he still presides over gastronomic juries and attends meetings with all the verve and appetite of a man half his age. This is the kidney dish with which Carnacina won a world-wide cooking competition in Paris in 1937; I give it as he tells it himself. He had only 8 minutes for the cooking but was allowed to prepare a few things in advance.

First of all Carnacina briefly fried a tablespoonful of chopped onion, with a pat of butter and a pinch of salt, and took it off the heat as soon as it began to brown. Then he did the same with a tablespoonful of chopped mushrooms, a pat of butter, and a pinch of salt. In another pan, he heated two liqueur glasses of cognac, set it alight, waited until it was reduced to half, and set it aside. All this belonged to the preparatory stage.

At the word Go – and you can have a try; I have myself scrupulously followed the Maestro's recipe – Carnacina put a good tablespoonful of butter in a saucepan, waited for it to foam before placing on top of it a good-sized (8 ounce) kidney which he had first dusted with flour. After 2½ minutes he turned it over, and waited another 2½ minutes; 5 minutes of the 8 had passed. He removed the kidney from the fire, sliced it up in a very hot soup plate, pulled out the spongy malodorous gristle inside, and left it where it would keep hot. Then he put another spoonful of butter in the pan, waited for it to foam, and added the cognac he had prepared before, then the onions and mushrooms, a drop of Worcestershire Sauce, a teaspoon-tip of mustard, pepper and salt; next he stirred them together, added the sliced kidney with the red juice that had drained into the soup plate, added another spoonful of already softened butter to keep the pan bottom from drying. Only a few seconds to go now – Carnacina squeezed in a few drops of lemon juice. Finished! And of course he won.

Kidney Omelette

Here is another way of enjoying kidneys. To make an omelette, you must soak the kidney for ½ hour in cold water to which a good splash of vinegar has been added; then dry and remove the outer membrane, slice it, pull out the spongy gristle in the centre, and set the kidney aside. Put a pan on to heat with a good pat of butter and a bruised clove of garlic (or 2 if you don't find them intimidating); when the garlic blanches, add 2–3 tablespoonfuls of green peas to the pan – a spoonful for each person. As they are cooking, beat up eggs in a bowl, 2 for every three people, then add a pinch of salt, a pinch of pepper, a tablespoonful of grated Parmesan for every 2 people, and finally the sliced kidney (the quantity depends on tastes; for some, a few slices are enough, but you can put quite a lot in as long as the ensemble is properly balanced by the egg).

Now back to the saucepan. The peas should be cooked. Remove the garlic and pour in the mixture of eggs and kidney. At this point the cooking should be more or less the same for any omelette, but there are one or two things to bear in mind.

First, the omelette will be much better if it is thick, so you will want a relatively small frying pan, with tall sides, to prevent the kidney from remaining on the surface.

Secondly, you will need a moderate flame to cook such a thick omelette as well as the kidney without toughening them.

Thirdly, don't forget to turn the omelette over when you see that the underside is done. It is very good served tepid, but even better when it's cold.

DIGRESSION
(The ineffable flavour)

Going back to the years of my early childhood during the war, I am more and more convinced that in spite of the horror and hardships of the period, I discovered two kinds of security upon which a child must absolutely depend: protection and food. It seems absurd now to speak of security when day after day, hour after hour, we were living under bombardment with the destruction of human lives, and were hungry from morning till night. But then in Pozzuoli, where I lived with my mother and grandparents, every day there acquired a ritual which managed to satisfy these different needs for security. Every evening we would wait for the last train to go by, then all the townsfolk would make for a long railway tunnel, where the next train would pass only at dawn the next morning. We would go in laden with blankets and any sort of rug we could lay our hands on to keep warm, make up our beds, and throw ourselves down to sleep. There was a hermetic heavy atmosphere among all that frightened humanity. But in those hours under the tunnel we felt protected not only because we felt safe from bombs but because we were all there, huddled up against one another, breathing the same air, trying to take heart and even finding enough space to play and have fun. It seemed to me there that I had gained an enormous family, my guardian angels had multiplied by the dozen, by the hundred. Today I understand that that tunnel, deep down, gave the peace and comfort a child feels in its mother's womb.

Now the other story was the story of my 'food'. At dawn we would be woken by shouts urging us to hurry, that soon the first train would be coming through. My mother would take me by the hand and hurry me along into the open country. In a certain place there was the wood fire of a goatherd among the caves and my mother would make for it, glancing furtively around at every step, so that nobody was on to her discovery. The goatherd would look at me with a sort of pity as he would have felt for a poor starved little lamb. He would milk one of his goats and a big mug of frothy goat's milk was handed to me, beautifully warm. I shall never forget the taste. It was unique. Warm, vital, restorative. I love good eating and I have eaten in almost every country in the world, exquisite dishes at the most sumptuous and fabulous tables, breathing in their fragrant, exotic smells, masterpieces of gastronomy, handed down through the generations. But no flavour will ever give me the confidence, the assurance of well-being, which I felt every morning in that foaming mug freshly milked from the goat. Probably I would have gone hungry for the day. But what did it matter? I was already living for the wonderful appointment of the following dawn.

I haven't told you about this episode to indulge in pathetic reminiscences. But even today I live on the lesson I learned in those days. That mug of milk has taught me that a food is good and downright unsurpassable when it harmonizes with its surroundings: the time, the place, the circumstances, the atmosphere, the sensation, the feelings – and above all – when it is absolutely genuine.

These reflections may seem a little out of place in a book of cooking recipes. But think about it: no, they are not really out of place. In fact they will help you to understand me better and my views on food and cooking.

Poultry and Game

I can't help wondering whether any of these recipes, especially the ones for turkey, could have anything new or original to say to the English and more especially the Americans, who are masters at cooking turkeys. Moreover it is to the American continent that Europeans owe this fat, richly flavoured bird. I am told that the Jesuits were the first to import it to Europe. Anway I should like to hand on the ways we do our turkeys and make them more widely known. I have also collected here a number of recipes for cooking pheasant of which I am particularly fond. One more point: you will notice that some of the recipes apply to rabbit as well as to chicken, because I wanted to avoid pointless repetition.

Chicken on the Spit

To cook chicken on the spit, the bird must be a good plump one: at least 3 pounds for 4 people, and, of course, cleaned and dressed. Brush the chicken lavishly with olive oil and let it rest for a few hours. Then stuff it with a seasoning made of a good slice of ham, a clove of garlic, 2 or 3 leaves of sage, a pinch of fennel seed, then one of salt and one of pepper. All these ingredients must be chopped up extremely fine and well blended. After the bird is stuffed, close any openings and rub the chicken all over with a cut clove of garlic, then drape with tissue-thin slices of ham, the fatter the better. Tie the bird up like a package so that the ham stays in place, and balance it on a spit. Roast slowly, over a low wood fire, if possible, which is the best of all.

Pollo alla Diavola
(Devilled Chicken)

Nobody really knows why this chicken is named after the prince of darkness. Perhaps because of the way it is cooked, on an open fire, smashed quite flat, so that the fowl has no further hope of salvation (but even so, it does attain a rare, crunchy perfection). At all events, the chicken should be a broiler weighing about 1 lb. 8 oz., really well cleaned (allow 1 chicken for each 2 people). Then, cut the bird in half leaving only half an inch or so still joined at the top to prevent its coming completely apart; next, flatten it on a wooden board by whacking it hard but taking care not to break the bones. Grease it all over with olive oil, then sprinkle with salt and pepper (a better idea is to add pepper and salt to the oil before the greasing). Finally, lay the chicken on a grill to roast over a fierce flame – a wood fire, if possible. After about 10 minutes on each side, the chicken will emerge golden and crunchy. You can also broil in the oven, about 5 inches from the flame, in which case you add a spig of rosemary and a splash of dry white wine before cooking.

Chicken (or Rabbit) alla Cacciatoro with Pimientos

This is a very familiar dish in Italy, but the addition of pimientos is strictly Neapolitan. Have a 3-pound chicken cleaned and cut into pieces as for frying. Place all in one large saucepan with 4–5 tablespoonfuls of olive oil (there was a time when you added dripping for flavour; and today there are still people who substitute a pat of butter if they are out of dripping, but olive oil is really just as good). Now add a sliced onion, a sprig of rosemary and a sprinkling of pepper and salt. Cook on a high flame. When the pieces of chicken are browning, add ¾ pint of coarsely cut tomatoes and ½ pint of pimientos, which have been well seeded and cut into strips. Cook for about 25–30 minutes on a moderate fire until the pimientos are soft and the chicken tender. If you don't use pimientos and increase the quantity of tomatoes by about ½ pint, you will have the classical *cacciatora.* But I find the pimientos lend splendour to the dish.

This should be enough for 4 persons.

Chicken as Porchetta

It was in Romagna again, the time I was filming *Boccaccio '70* that I found this wonderful recipe. Porchetta as you now know, is a young pig stuffed with herbs and roasted, as they do in Rome. Well, this chicken tastes amazingly like it.

Have a 3–3 lb. 8 oz. chicken dressed but not cut up (it will serve 4 people). Then make a stuffing with about 8 ounces of diced ham, 1 tablespoonful or so of ham fat or lard, the giblets of the same bird minced (and, if possible, of another as well), the spiky leaves of a sprig of rosemary, a little wild fennel, a minced clove of garlic and a pinch each of pepper and salt. Mix them all well and stuff the chicken. Then tie it up and roast in a pan with a little olive oil and another sprig of rosemary. It will take a little over an hour in a moderate oven (375°F).

Chicken (or rabbit) Fricassée

This recipe takes us to Tuscany – and a memory of quite a few years back. I was making a film with Marcello Mastroianni and Vittorio De Sica, a very animated scene from *La Bella Mugnaia* (*The Miller's Beautiful Wife*). Owing to all the excitement, I managed to break the mirror which my make-up man was handing me between takes. It was quite a tragedy. I'm not nearly so superstitious today as I was then, but in those days I was – horribly. I spent a terrible day; and to be brutally honest there wasn't a soul in the company who was above *all that*, nobody capable of persuading me how silly I was to worry about such nonsense. I realized to my horror that everyone else in the company was just as superstitious as I was. That evening my nerves were completely worn to shreds after waiting all day for the disaster (which fortunately never occurred) and I went in very reluctantly to dinner. And that was the occasion when I met the chicken whose recipe I am now giving you. It came to the table with such a ravishing smell, looking so irresistible, that I began to eat slowly, then more and more greedily, with deep, deep satisfaction. So I thank God for that Tuscan chicken fricassée, because it said more to me than a many a good talking-to from wise friends. As I went on eating I gradually emerged from that miasma of dread, my spirits soared, and I felt bold enough to break another ten mirrors without batting an eyelid. Today I couldn't absolutely swear that it was only the chicken fricassée that worked the miracle. But the fact remains, and I have never, never fallen out of love with that chicken. And I know you'll love it, too, so here is the recipe.

For 4 persons, have a 3–3 lb. 8 oz. chicken cleaned and cut into eight pieces. Brown in a heavy pan in 2–3 tablespoonfuls each of olive oil and butter and a whole peeled onion. As the pieces of chicken brown, take them out of the pan, and remove the onion. To the remaining oil and butter, add 2 tablespoonfuls of flour, about ¾ pint of chicken stock, and a sprinkling of salt and pepper. Stir, then replace the pieces of chicken (not the onion, as its work is done) and add 2 tablespoonfuls of chopped mushrooms (better fresh, but if you have to use dried, first revive them for an hour or so in warm water). Cover and wait for the mushrooms to cook and begin to disintegrate; this will take about half an hour. By then the pieces of chicken will be just about done. This is when you whisk up 4 egg yolks in a bowl, pour into the pan with the rest, give it one last stir, then serve.

The dish will be even better if you make it this way: First transfer the pieces of chicken from the pan to the serving dish, then add the eggs to the sauce, then pour the sauce over the pieces of chicken.

Variation: Rabbit can be used instead of chicken. Prepare the recipe in exactly the same way.

Chicken Curry

I was initiated into Indian cooking when I was in London and the friends I was with, all experts in the field, said it was every bit as good as in New Delhi, or Rangoon, or Ceylon. And I loved it, as it has so much common ground with my own native Mediterranean cooking only the flavours are more varied, stronger and sweeter. I also discovered that there are at least a dozen ways of making chicken curry. As I always ask for the recipes of the things I like most, I chose this one.

Fry a thinly sliced onion and chopped clove of garlic in 3 tablespoonfuls olive oil for a few minutes. Then mix in ¼ pint of coconut milk, half a grated coconut, 1 teaspoonful of coriander, a teaspoonful of prepared mustard, ½ teaspoonful of saffron (the original recipe has a whole but I prefer to reduce the saffron), ½ teaspoonful of powdered cumin, half a minced chilipepper (or less if you aren't used to them), and an abundant sprinkling of pepper. Cook this mixture for a few minutes to form a thick sauce, and finally add a 3-pound chicken which has been cut into pieces and nicely browned in olive oil. Now turn down the flame, cover the pan, and leave to finish cooking; it will take about half an hour. Look at it from time to time. If the sauce has become too thick and sticks to the bottom of the pan, add a spoonful or two of stock or warm water. Right at the very end, before taking the curry from the heat, give it a sprinkling of salt and stir in the juice of half a lemon. This recipe serves 4 persons.

Boiled Capon

A capon is certainly a better fowl to boil than a hen because it has more meat on the bone, will cook more tenderly and make better stock. Otherwise, this recipe works perfectly well for chicken.

Buy a clean and dressed capon (a 6-pound bird will serve 6–8). Before putting the capon in the pot, sew the cavities shut and truss it so that it keeps its shape. Fill the pot with cold water until the capon is well covered, then throw in an onion stuck with a clove, a carrot, a stick of celery and very little salt. Put the lid on and let the capon cook on a moderate heat, skimming the froth off from time to time. The cooking will take about an hour and a half. Serve capon cut in pieces, and accompany with something very tasty to complement the delicate flavour. I would recommend a green sauce or a caper sauce or something similar. Real gourmets, however, put the ultimate finishing touch over the pieces of boiled capon: as it lies before them on the table, they sprinkle over it a few grains of coarse kitchen salt.

Stuffed boiled Capon

This is prepared in exactly the same way as the simple boiled capon. But it is stuffed and the ingredients vary.

Trim crusts from 6 slices of bread, then dip slices in milk and wring out so that bread is no more than moist; then add the livers and giblets cooked in stock and cut up fine, a chopped onion fried quickly in butter without browning, 2 eggs, 3–4 ounces of minced ham, a pinch of nutmeg and a pinch each of salt and pepper. Mix well and use to stuff the capon. Sew the bird up, truss, and boil as described. Serve cut into pieces, with the stuffing sliced in the centre of the dish. Accompany it with green sauce or caper sauce, or vegetables cooked in the stock.

Stuffed Guinea-Hen with Rice

The female guinea-fowl is a queen of the Italian dinner table, especially in the Po Valley where it still rivals the turkey. Normally the recipes for one bird can be used for the other (with changes in proportions, of course, because guineas weigh about as much as a small chicken). This recipe is a special one for guinea-hen only.

For 6 people you will need 3 guinea-hens weighing 2–2 lb. 8 oz. each. Prepare the hens as all poultry: pluck, clean the insides, remove the heads and entrails, tweeze out the quills, and singe off any hairs. Then wash birds well, dry, grease the insides with a very small quantity of butter, sprinkle with salt and pepper and stuff with stuffing.

For the stuffing: slowly boil 1 cup of rice in just enough milk to cover it at the outset; as the milk is absorbed, you should very slowly add more until the rice is boiled al dente. It should take about 1 pint of milk. Now mix 3–4 ounces of finely chopped walnuts with 3–4 ounces of crumbled roasted chestnuts (previously shelled) 7 ounces each of grated Parmesan, breadcrumbs and diced truffles, a chopped sprig of parsley, one egg, a pinch of nutmeg, and one of pepper and salt. Work all these ingredients together with the rice into a paste that is solid without being excessively creamy, then stuff the guinea-hens. Don't pack the stuffing in too tightly, as it must have room to expand as the birds cook. Wrap any left-over stuffing in foil so that it can be baked separately in a slow oven. Sew the birds up, wrap round them a few slices of pork fat, tie in place with string, and brown the birds all over in a little olive oil, butter, and pork fat with a couple of coarsely chopped onions. After 15 minutes, add about ¾ pint of dry white wine, cover, and cook slowly. Check the pan now and then, and if it is drying up spoon in a little chicken stock. When the guinea-hens are done (after 1–1½ hours), cut in pieces, and arrange them on a serving dish around the slices of stuffing. (Also, don't forget to serve the foil-wrapped stuffing.) Finally, strain the juice and pour it over the birds. If you want to add one last exquisite touch, thicken the sauce (after it is sieved) with a tablespoonful of flour, then put it back in the pan and liven it up with a small glass of cognac.

Roast Turkey

The recipe for roast turkey is, in fact most recipes for roast turkey are, almost exactly identical with recipes for roast pheasant or chicken on the spit. The only difference lies in its slower and gentler cooking on the fire owing to its bulk. It is because of its dimensions that I prefer stuffed turkey. The English and Americans, I know, are masters of roasting turkeys. But now I would like to mention an Italian recipe. This is the way they cook their Christmas turkeys in Milan.

It must first, of course, be well cleaned and dressed; better still if it is a tender young turkey hen which is easier to cook and juicier, and weighing under 5 pounds. You make the stuffing with 1 pound of roasted chestnuts, peeled and crumbled, 2 peeled, sliced apples, 2 peeled, sliced pears, a scant 8 ounces of minced stoned prunes; a scant 8 ounces of a long thin sausage which the Milanese call *luganega*, also minced; a small white truffle cut into slivers, a pinch of pepper and salt. All these ingredients must be well mixed, but you should not overdo the pounding and crushing. Each should be allowed to breathe individually and form a sort of rainbow of flavours. When they are mixed to your satisfaction, leave the filling for a few hours in a bowl and macerate it with about ¾ pint of dry white wine; and some people also add a small glass of cognac. Now stuff your turkey, sew it up, and place it in a roasting pan greased with butter and rubbed with a few sage leaves and a sprig of rosemary. The roasting takes quite a long time, at least 3 hours in a moderate oven (375°F.). Every now and then ladle up the juice that collects in the pan and use it to baste the turkey. Serve it sliced with its drippings sieved and poured over the top.

Stuffed Breast of Turkey

You may prefer to stuff only the breast of a turkey; the recipe is again one from Milan.

First you clean and lightly pound a boned breast of turkey on a wooden board as though it were a large beefsteak (many butchers will do the boning for you). Then, allowing a small margin around the edge, spread over the breast a mixture of the following: 10 ounces of minced veal (for a large breast), 2 good slices of ham, minced, a beaten egg, 2 tablespoonfuls of Parmesan cheese and a sliver of truffle, minced. All these must be worked up into a thick and fairly homogeneous paste.

Now roll the turkey breast round it to form a sort of salami, wrap it in cheesecloth, tying at the ends, and cook in a large heavy saucepan of water. (The water should come about one inch over the turkey.) Into the water put a good pinch of salt, some sage and thyme leaves, a sprig of rosemary and a clove-studded onion. It will take the turkey 2 hours to cook in simmering water. Finally, unwrap and slice, then serve with boiled spinach with mixed sultanas and pine nuts, or any other kind of boiled vegetable.

As an added refinement, chill the cooked slices of turkey breast and glaze with a coating of aspic.

Turkey Breast alla Bolognese

For this recipe you must cut the boned turkey breast in two or even four parts according to the size, so that each piece represents one portion. Clean, then flatten each piece into the shape of an escalope by pounding; dip into beaten egg, then breadcrumbs, and brown in butter over a high flame. Immediately afterwards, place on each piece a thin slice of ham with a good streak of fat to it, and on top of the ham a slice of Parmesan cheese. Pack all the pieces closely together in a baking dish and put them into a very hot oven for one minute only. If you are interested in cutting down on calories, you can also use a softer cheese with a more delicate taste.

Roast Pheasant

I can't resist mentioning that pheasant, done in every possible way, has been my passion as long as I have had my farm, Tenuta dell'Occhio, my Ticino hideaway a few miles from the Po. The very first day I went there with my husband and our little Carlo we were engulfed by a mighty cloud of brilliantly beating wings: literally thousands of pheasants. The gamekeeper told me that in full season there are around eight thousand pheasants living, roosting, and breeding on the farm. You can always see the young pheasants and young hares crossing the roads and the pathways and guests are warned to drive very cautiously in their cars.

I now have such a treasury of pheasant recipes that I hardly know where to start. So I may as well begin with the simplest.

First of all, a few words about an old bone of contention. They say, it is a well-known fact, that a pheasant must always be hung: but what does this word mean exactly? How long should the hanging take? Some say 3 or 4 days, others say 7 or 8. I find the best way is between the two. The pheasant must be hung long enough for the meat to tenderize to the right consistency, but not so long as to acquire that strong smell of 'high' game which some people claim to cherish, for reasons that have remained a mystery to me. These gourmets always seem a little over-anxious to indulge in out-of-the-way sensations of the table. I say a pheasant should be hung 5 or 6 days at the very most. And in the fresh air, hooked by the head. Naturally it alters the case if the pheasant is hung in the refrigerator. You will certainly need a day or so longer. But then that isn't a natural process.

Having said all this, few things are so simple as roasting a pheasant. For 4 persons, choose a 2 lb. 8 oz.–3 lb. bird. You must first clean it very well, pluck it and singe away the remaining hairs and fluff. Wash off any dirt, then dry, and season with a mince of bacon, ham fat, and a few sage leaves. (This is not a stuffing proper, but a sort of grease to be rubbed over the inside of the bird, a scant 4 ounces at the maximum.) Sprinkle, too, with salt and pepper, then sew the bird up, truss, and drape it with a few thin slices of ham; put it in a baking pan greased with olive oil to roast in a moderate oven (350–375°F.). When it is half done (you need 50–60 minutes altogether), sprinkle with dry white wine.

Stewed Pheasant

Clean and prepare the pheasant as above, cutting it into 8 pieces. Have ready a stuffing of salt pork (2 ounces), a thinly sliced onion, a chopped carrot and stick of celery, and a pinch of nutmeg. Sauté the stuffing in a heavy saucepan and, when it blanches, add the pieces of pheasant; wait for them to take on colour, then sprinkle with salt and pepper. When the pheasant is a golden brown, splash with about a wineglassful of marsala or a good cognac, cover and continue to cook slowly. It should take about 40–45 minutes. If you notice that the pan is drying up, spoon in a little stock. When the pheasant is cooked, arrange the pieces on a serving dish, strain the juices, and pour on top.

VARIATION: One very refined variation is to add a spoonful of crumbled black truffle to the juices a little before the pheasant is done. Or else drop slivers of truffle, black or white, over the pheasant in the serving dish.

Fagiano alla Creta
(Pheasant Baked in Clay)

This recipe comes from the Po Valley. They say that it goes back more than a thousand years to the time of the Longobardi, ancestors of the Lombards. As you need a large lump of salt clay to bake the pheasant in, the bird shouldn't be too large. A young 2-pound hen is the most suitable, and much tenderer to cook. It will serve 2 persons.

Prepare your pheasant, a young pheasant hen, in the way described. Then spread over the kitchen table a large sheet of greaseproof paper. On the paper put a layer of thin slices of fatty bacon; then spread the bacon with butter, and cover with a pounded mixture of herbs such as rosemary, thyme, mint, juniper, etc.; sprinkle with salt and pepper. Over this foundation lay your pheasant, wrap it up carefully in the paper and seal. Then completely cover it with about 1 lb. 8 oz. of soft potter's clay (you must, however, make absolutely sure that the wall of clay is the same thickness all round and that there are no holes or weak spots). Put it in the oven – at least 325°F. – for 2½ hours. Take it out of the oven, smash off the clay which will have baked into pottery, rip off the paper, throw away the flavourings and herbs, and the pheasant will emerge with all its bouquet and flavour intact.

Pheasant Casserole with Chestnuts

Clean and dress a 2-pound pheasant. Put 3 table-spoonfuls of chopped salt pork in a saucepan with a pat of butter, 1 tablespoonful of olive oil, a carrot, an onion, a stick of celery, a handful of parsley, all chopped fine. Let them blanch over a high flame. On top of them put your pheasant. Wait for it to brown on all sides (this will take about half an hour), then splash it with about a wineglassful of dry white wine and ¼ pint of chicken stock. Cover, and allow it to cook slowly for another half an hour. Meanwhile, boil 10 ounces of shelled chestnuts. When they are cooked, pull away the inner skin, put them back in the pan with 1 pint of milk, a pinch of salt, and one of sugar. When the chestnuts begin to disintegrate, put them through a sieve, return them to the stove with what remains of their cooking milk, and when the mixture thickens, stir it well with a wooden spoon. Then pour it into the centre of the serving dish, surround it with the pheasant, cut into pieces, and moisten with the strained juices from the pan.

Duck and Orange

This is probably the most famous dish in the world: but everywhere I have eaten it, I have discovered a different version. In France it is one of the national glories. Florentines appeal to history for proof that they invented it, as it is mentioned in the annals of the fifteenth century. As far as I am concerned the best duck and orange I have ever tasted was at Aylesbury in Buckinghamshire. At the time I was filming *The Key* with William Holden and Trevor Howard. The director, Sir Carol Reed, invited me to a restaurant there, with the solemn promise that I was going to eat the most incredible duck and orange in the world. And I did – three helpings of it. And in spite of the fact that I've had it time and time again at the tables of the most food-conscious people I know, I have never again found anything like the flavour of the duck and orange of Aylesbury. Unfortunately at the time I didn't ask the chef for the recipe. But ever after I have never failed to dig the recipes out of people and compare the ones of several great chefs: then I have experimented on my own. Here is the one that I now consider the best:

To start with the duck mustn't be fully grown and hardened by its life at liberty, but it should be a duckling, of about 4 pounds, a *caneton*. For 6 people, at least 2 ducks should be cooked as one wouldn't supply enough meat for the group. You prepare them (or have them prepared) the same way as you would any roast poultry: clean them well, cutting off the head, the feet, plucking the feathers, etc. Then grease them inside and out with butter, sprinkle with salt, prick the skin well all over so that the ducklings give up some of their own fat, and roast them in a hot oven (425–450°F.) in a butter-greased roasting pan for about 25 minutes. Lower the oven temperature and continue roasting for 1–1½ hours.

Before the ducklings are quite roasted, take them out of the oven and put them aside where they will keep hot. And keep the juices that have collected in the pan. At the same time that the ducklings are roasting, make the sauce: wash and peel a good-sized orange, discarding the white pith; cut the peel into strips and boil it in water for 4 or 5 minutes; drain, dry, and cool the peel, then let it macerate a couple of hours in a tablespoonful of curaçao.

Now back to the pan in which you have cooked your ducklings. Add to the juices in the bottom 4 tablespoonfuls of a good brown meat stock, strained and skimmed of fat (for this you really need what chefs call a brown *fondo* of veal, but if you have none, you can use a good beef consommé), add a good pinch of potato flour (or plain flour), and 3 tablespoonfuls of dry sherry. Cook over a hot flame, stirring steadily to keep the sauce from lumping. Then return the ducklings to the pan; immediately add the slivers of orange peel with the curaçao and the juice of 1 orange; continue cooking for a while and stirring on the top of the stove until the ingredients bind.

Finally, take the ducklings from the pan, cut them into quarters, arrange on a platter and cover them with their sauce. Around them set quarters of two completely peeled oranges, with the thin membrane removed from the juicy flesh. I know it is complicated, but then it is a real *caneton à l'orange*. Otherwise it is better to do without and tackle something simpler, don't you think?

Roast Goose

A goose is fatter than a guinea-hen or a turkey, so the problem of cooking it whole is more complicated. However, somebody taught me this recipe, which gets round all the difficulties. And it is worthwhile, because the fatness of the goose makes its meat cook deliciously.

The solution of the problem lies in not actually making a stuffing for the goose but in giving it a seasoning which will help to cook and flavour it at the same time. You prepare this seasoning by frying in a pan a thinly chopped onion with 3 tablespoonfuls of butter. When the onion blanches, take the pan from the fire and add the chopped liver of the goose, a few little sage leaves, a sprinkling of salt, one of pepper, a pinch of nutmeg and one of cloves. Put the pan back on the heat for a few minutes, and stir together so that it forms a very thick paste which will do for greasing. First grease the inside of the goose with butter, then smear it with the liver paste; sew it up, tie with string and wrap the goose in a sheet of greaseproof paper previously rubbed with butter and sprinkled with salt. Finally, put the goose on the spit and cook it about 20–25 minutes for each pound over a low heat or in a slow oven. (An 8- or 9-pound goose is a good size for 6 people.) During the last quarter of an hour, you remove the paper (which was meant to concentrate the heat and allow it to penetrate inside the bird). Now expose the goose to direct heat so that the skin turns crisp and brown.

Roast Quail

Wash, clean, and pluck 1 bird for each person to be served. Then grease the insides of the quails with butter, sprinkle with salt and pepper. If you have a truffle handy, place a small chunk inside each of the birds. Sprinkle the outside with salt and pepper, wrap the quails in very thin slices of salt pork and then in small sheets of greaseproof paper. (If you can insert a vine leaf between the greaseproof paper and the fat, it will bestow the most delicious flavour.) Now cook the quails very carefully in a moderate oven (375°F.), allowing 50–60 minutes for each pound. Shortly before they are done, tear off the paper and finally the vine leaf, so that the skin will become crisp and brown.

Partridges

Clean and pluck the partridges, one for every person, and lightly grease the insides with butter; sprinkle with pepper and salt, place one sage leaf inside each bird; lay a slice of pork fat across each breast, attaching it firmly with a thread or string. Brown the partridges in butter in a pan over a high flame, then reduce the flame, splash the bottom of the pan with dry white wine (about ½–¾ pint); add two bay leaves, cover and cook slowly for 30–45 minutes until tender. When the partridges are cooked, remove them from the pan and keep them hot.

Meanwhile put the livers, cut in pieces, in the juices remaining in the pan (with a few more livers, too, if you have them, otherwise chicken livers) and cook for less than a minute, so that they keep their flavour; the sauce is now ready to pour on the partridges. As a last touch: a few slivers of truffle.

Rabbit in Sweet and Sour Sauce

You can cook rabbit in just about any way that you cook chicken, and we have already looked at some of them. But now I want to show you another way which is purely for rabbit, and it couldn't be simpler.

For 4 persons, you will need a 2–3 pound rabbit. The rabbit is skinned, cleaned, washed, and cut into pieces. Then you fry up 2 sliced onions in 3–4 tablespoonfuls olive oil, into which you put the pieces of rabbit after dipping them very lightly in flour. When they begin to brown, splash them lightly with vinegar and repeat two or three times, gradually adding a rounded tablespoonful of sultanas, a tablespoonful of sugar, a heaped tablespoonful of pine nuts, a sprinkling of salt and pepper, and a sprig of thyme. Some people use only vinegar, others a mixture of half vinegar and half dry white wine (about a wineglass of each; if you use only vinegar ¼ pint is ample). Finish the cooking in a covered pot on a moderate flame (it will take about 1–1½ hours), then serve.

Neapolitan Rabbit with Sauce

This is my maternal grandmother's recipe. Here, too, the rabbit is skinned, cleaned, and cut into pieces. Heat in a pan with a little oil, a piece of lard or a little meat dripping (though the lard isn't essential, it was always used and gave the meat a livelier, softer taste). Then throw in 2 or 3 partly crushed cloves of garlic. When the garlic begins to brown, take it out, and put in the pieces of rabbit, lightly dipped in flour. Wait for them to start cooking, then splash them with about ½ pint of dry white wine. When the wine is reduced, throw in cut-up tomatoes (1 pound of tomatoes for a 2–3 pound rabbit, or more if you prefer); sprinkle with salt, paprika, or better still, add half a chilipepper which you should remember to remove at the end. You may even want to add a few black olives, stoned and chopped: choose which of the two appeals the more. Then cover and leave it to cook quietly for about 1–1½ hours until it is done. One rabbit will serve 4 people.

Lepre in Salmi
(Jugged Hare)

A hare needs to hang longer than other game. Eight days should be enough. Then you skin, clean, wash and cut it in pieces which must then marinate for 2 days (3 days are always better, however) in a cool place in a generous red wine with a clove-studded onion, a stick of celery, a carrot, a stick of cinnamon, a few bay leaves and a few peppercorns. At cooking time, you sauté half a sliced onion in a mixture of butter and minced pork fat (about 2 tablespoonfuls of each); put in your pieces of hare lightly dipped in flour; when the cooking is well under way and the hare nicely browned, add the vegetables which were in the marinade (previously sieved) and the liver of the hare finely chopped. Finally you cover with the wine of the marinade. From now on you let it bubble over a slow fire, until the wine is consumed and has formed a nice thick sauce. When the hare is cooked (this will take about 2 hours), lay the pieces in a serving dish, strain the sauce and pour it over the meat.

If the hare is a good-sized one, 5–6 pounds, this recipe will serve 8. I feel I should mention that this is my own personal variation on the classical recipe. I make it this way because it is not only more convenient but I like it. I hope you'll like it too.

DIGRESSION

(Husbands slaving over a hot stove)

Until a few years ago, every good mother of a family who gave her daughter advice on her wedding night never failed to make a point of urging her to 'take her husband by the throat', that is, to spoil him with treats, titbits, and special dishes. And she was convinced, that dear old mama, that the only way of 'preserving' a husband and tying him forever to his wife was to filter all the problems of married life through 'the throat and stomach'.

The concept has now become rather old-fashioned it's true, swept away by the new liberality which has fortunately been introduced into the life of a modern couple. But the fundamental truth remains intact. So now one can say that it holds good for both sides. The husband nowadays can bring about an effective rehabilitation, smooth over a misunderstanding, a wrinkle on the bridal bow by 'taking his wife by the throat'. So let the husband get busy at the stove once in a while and enjoy himself cooking at least a few really successful dishes of his own. Now *there's* a handsome picture of domestic bliss.

The men who consider themselves 'old-fashioned' but who have in fact learned nothing from the past, and as regards the present simply refuse to recognize that the woman works and takes part in every field of social activity – such men will be irritated, if not scandalized, by my attitude. 'What?' they will say. 'A man in an apron? Slaving at the stove like a good little housewife!' In fact they are the ones whose ideas lag sadly behind the evolution of society, who have most need of therapeutic cooking. The family circles of men with those ideas must be swarming with problems!

And it is to them, these husbands who are still up in arms at the idea of the modern woman, that I deliver my invitation to hunt through these recipes of mine and try one or two. They will be grateful, I'll bet anything on that.

As the greater number of my readers are bound to be women, to them I say: enjoy cooking! And don't let it develop into a dull routine. You will like it and it will not be a dreary chore as long as you are proud to have cooked something which your husband and your children will compliment you on. Believe me, it is a system which will cut down your visits to the psychiatrist.

Eggs and Vegetables

You can do many things with eggs and vegetables, especially when you get your imagination to work and let the ideas for original dishes just come.

For me, the success of a dish is not only due to the fact that it is well made; anybody can do that. A good dish is often a spontaneous creation in the kitchen, not the least of its charm being that it is one right off the record! Naturally these vegetable dishes are only accompaniments to the main course, but I prefer to regard them as complete in themselves. There are some vegetable dishes, ways of doing aubergines, pimientos, and so on, that sometimes fill me with an enthusiasm that I am unable to work up over the main courses.

Eggs in Tomato Sauce

Make the tomato sauce (which I have given for spaghetti), with 1 pound of tomatoes, 3 tablespoonfuls of olive oil, a teaspoonful of tomato purée, a half onion sliced thin, salt and pepper, and some leaves of basil. Into this sauce drop 6 eggs, taking care not to break the yolks: it will all be ready in a few minutes. You can scramble the eggs in the sauce; in which case you would eat them on toast. Serves 6 people.

Curried Eggs

Allow 2 hard-boiled eggs for each person. Shell the eggs and cut in halves lengthwise, removing the yolks. The yolks are then sieved and mixed with a Béchamel sauce. I shan't go on to describe this famous sauce, but merely remind you that it is made from butter melted in a pan and blended with flour, boiling milk, salt and pepper, and, in our case, a good helping of curry powder. (The quantity depends on how much you like curry.) Mix in and blend the yolks, which will make a filling to stuff the empty whites. Arrange your egg halves very close together in a fireproof dish, cover with more Béchamel, and bake for 10 minutes in a moderately hot oven (350°F.).

Courgette Omelètte

This is a daily dish that nobody ever seems to get tired of in Rome. This is how I have been taught to make it, according to centuries of tradition.

Wash 4 ounces, say, of courgettes and cut them into thin slices; then cook them in a pan with a tablespoonful of olive oil, which you should gradually dilute with a tablespoonful of water to keep the vegetable juicy and soft.

Beat 6 eggs, pour the courgettes into them, then add a pinch each of salt, pepper, and chopped parsley, and pour everything into a large frying pan with about 2 tablespoonfuls of olive oil; cook the omelette, turning it over when the underside is crisp. This omelette is normally cooked in olive oil, but it is even more delicious when fried in bacon or meat dripping.

Courgette Flower Omelette

If the courgette omelette is an everyday delight for the Romans, the one made with courgette (vegetable marrow) flowers is a rare and sublime experience. The preparation is almost the same, but I have seen it turn out more successfully if instead of cooking the flowers whole, you tear them up into pieces of more or less equal size. Cook them in a pan with olive oil and a sprinkling of salt, then pour them into the beaten egg without forgetting to add a good pinch of chopped parsley. Then turn everything into the frying pan.

Artichoke Omelette

Another Roman speciality and one of the best. For 6 persons, take 2 or 3 plump baby artichokes, clean them, cut off the spiky leaves, remove the chokes and cut into quarters. Before cooking the artichokes, let them stand a few minutes in a bowl of cold water and squeeze in the juice of a lemon to prevent them from going black. Now cook them in a frying pan or omelette pan with 2 tablespoonfuls of olive oil (or dripping according to the century-old method), salt, pepper, and a dash of water if the pan threatens to cook dry. When the artichokes are cooked, leave the frying pan on the fire and pour in 6 beaten eggs and a good pinch of chopped parsley. Leave it on the stove a few minutes longer, so that the eggs cook and mix with the artichokes. The omelette is ready.

Aubergine 'Mushrooms'

This is one of the easiest ways of doing aubergine, and the result will be a vegetable which will add a breath of vitality to anything it is served with. For 4 persons you will need 2 small aubergines.

Cut them in long strips, leaving the skin on, but removing the central part with the seeds. Then cut the strips into small chunks (like mushrooms) which you sauté in olive oil. There mustn't be much oil in the pan because the aubergine should remain a little dry and crisp. Before putting it in, heat the oil with 2 or 3 cloves of crushed garlic. Add the aubergine and cook over a moderate heat with a sprinkling of salt and pepper. Finally, throw in a handful of chopped parsley.

VARIATION: A successful variation which gives a lift to the flavour of the vegetable is to add a few slices of tomato as the aubergine is cooking.

Roast Aubergine

For 4 people you will need one medium to large aubergine. Begin by cleaning it thoroughly without removing the skin, but do slice off the stem end. Then cut the aubergine in half lengthwise and dig out the seeds, disturbing the flesh as little as possible. Afterwards, make a series of criss-cross incisions down the length of each half to facilitate cooking. Add a sprinkling of salt and pepper and spread over both halves a pinch of very finely chopped garlic. Now grease a baking dish with olive oil, pack the aubergine halves tightly inside, the skin down and flesh side up, trickle a little more oil over them, and bake in a moderate oven (375°F.) until tender, about 30–40 minutes.

Crumbled Aubergine

Slice the aubergine, lengthwise, each slice no thicker than about ¼ inch, but certainly no thinner. Then sprinkle slices with salt on a large plate, put another plate on top with a heavy object on it to weight it down. The slices have to be weighted, with salt, to let out their bitter juice. (The Neapolitans have an amusingly vulgar expression for it which normally has nothing whatever to do with the kitchen!) Leave the aubergine for 2 or 3 hours, then wash the slices and dry them. At this point, each slice is dipped into beaten egg yolk, then into flour and fried in olive oil just until crusty and golden. Delicious! One medium-sized aubergine will serve 4 people.

Aubergine *a Scapece*

Scapece is the system of marinating used in southern Italy. For 4 people allow a medium-sized aubergine. Slice it rather thickly or in quarters and parboil in boiling salted water, being careful to take it out while the pulp is still a bit crisp, in about 5 minutes. Then dry the aubergine well, in fact you should press out the water that has soaked in, but without breaking the slices. Let these cool, then put them into a large shallow bowl, season with 5 tablespoonfuls of olive oil and 2–3 tablespoonfuls vinegar, a sprinkling of salt, one of oregano, a couple of finely sliced cloves of garlic, some peppercorns or, better still, a few pieces of chilipepper. Stir once or twice, cover the bowl, set in a cool place and leave alone for 1 or, even better 2 days.

Fried Pimientos

This is the simplest way of cooking pimientos (or sweet red peppers), and yet even for us Neapolitans it is always something of a treat. You simply cut the pimientos into strips, after first seeding and coring, then cook them in deep heated olive oil, sprinkle with salt, and shake off the drops of oil. (But keep some for flavour!)

Pimientos Fried with Capers and Olives

This is the richest version I know of fried pimientos. You start out as before, cutting pimientos into strips, and frying them in a pan with about 1 inch of hot olive oil: but stop before the pimientos are quite cooked. Take them out and drain them, pour off a part of the oil in the pan; put the pimientos back so that they are *a puccia* as we say (that is, in enough oil), but without splashing. Start to fry them again, adding 1 finely chopped clove of garlic (for 2 pounds of pimientos which will serve 4–6); a tablespoonful or two, according to taste, of capers, a handful of black olives, stoned and cut in pieces. Towards the end add a sprinkling of pepper and a handful of chopped parsley.

Roast Pimientos

There are, of course, people who prefer roast pimientos to fried because this way it is easier to remove the outer skin, which improves the taste considerably. But you have to know the proper technique. Here it is. Roast the pimientos exactly as they are, on an open grill or in a hot oven; then wrap them in a sheet of greaseproof paper and let them cool. It is then easy to peel off the outer skin, without getting the pimientos wet (which makes them lose flavour); you only have to dip your finger-tips in water from time to time. Now you have only the pure flesh of the pimiento, which you proceed to cut into strips and season with oil, basil, and capers. All this you can do with raw pimientos, or those heated for a *minimum* time in a frying pan *without* any oil.

Pimientos stuffed with Aubergine

There are many ways of making stuffed pimientos, and each of them is good. The classic filling is made of bread-crumbs, sultanas, pine nuts, and so on. But the one I love is this one:

First of all, for 4 people, roast 4 large pimientos as described in the recipe for Roast Pimientos, then gently pull off the outer skin. You then cook 2 small or 1 medium aubergine in 'mushroom' style, according to the Aubergine Mushrooms recipe, but instead of frying only with olive oil, garlic, and parsley, you add capers and chopped black olives, about 1 rounded tablespoonful of each, to add to the range of flavours, and, if you wish, an anchovy fillet, rinsed free of salt and minced. This is now the filling to stuff into the pimientos, which are then packed tightly in a baking dish. Pour a little oil over them and bake for a few minutes in a hot oven.

Pimientos stuffed with Spaghetti

This one, too, couldn't be more Neapolitan, or easier to make. Roast the pimientos as described, peel them, and fill with cooked spaghetti; season with tomato sauce and pieces of Mozzarella cheese and leave them to cool. Later, pack pimientos tightly in a baking dish, spoon a good dollop of olive oil on top of each, add a sprinkling of salt, and bake in a moderate oven for about 20 minutes until good and hot.

Tarato

This is a Greek dish, which I discovered when we were filming *Boy on a Dolphin* on Hydra. You make it with roasted pimientos and roasted aubergine, about equal quantities of each.

The pimientos are roasted whole on an open grill, then very slowly and carefully the outer skin is peeled away. You can cut the aubergine into fat slices, cook in a little olive oil until tender but still firm and then peel their skin off, too. Now cut the pulp of both vegetables very fine, mix in a bowl with the addition of a large helping of yoghurt. Beat into a thick paste. Then add garlic, pounded to pulp in a mortar, salt, pepper, a trickle of olive oil, and a little lemon juice.

In the hot summer nights by the Aegean, an excellently roasted fish, followed by a slice of the local bread and Tarato was bliss.

Onions in Sweet and Sour Sauce

For this you need those fresh, juicy, tender little white onions. You start off by putting 1 tablespoonful of dripping or melted pork fat into a pan. To this add 1–2 tablespoonfuls of minced ham fat, a few chopped baby onions, and a chopped clove of garlic. The proportions of these ingredients are optional, the main thing is to make a highly flavoured base. Now put in the whole peeled onions (allowing 3 for each person; to keep from being overpowered by the fumes as you peel the onions, soak them first in cold running water for a few hours). When the onions blanch, add a little sugar, then water and vinegar (half and half) to cover the onions. Let the liquid boil down until the onions remain in only a light sauce: they are ready.

Beans in Tomato Sauce

Green beans make a perfect accompaniment to many dishes if you can find the time to sit down and string them and cut off the tips to avoid that tangle of fibres in your teeth. If you do have the time, the worst is over.

Boil the beans, trimmed and strung (about 1 pound for 4 people), in plenty of lightly salted water. Meanwhile, put into a pan a little lard, pork fat, butter, or olive oil (some kind of fat to partly fry a sliced onion in). To this add a sliced or chopped tomato; after a quarter of an hour add the beans, well drained of their water. As they are just cooking, season with salt, pepper, and chopped parsley. 5 to 10 minutes more and that's all there is to it.

Baby Carrots in Egg Sauce

You must have tender, very young carrots. Pare them with a knife (a pound of them for 3–4 people), wash, dry, and put into a saucepan with a tablespoonful of butter. Then add about ½ pint of meat or chicken stock, and also about a teaspoonful of flour, a pinch of chopped parsley and about ⅛ teaspoonful of nutmeg. Put the lid on and let the carrots cook over a low heat without coming to the boil. When the carrots are tender and a good sauce has formed around them (this will take about 15 minutes), take the saucepan from the stove; mix a little hot sauce into an egg yolk that has been whisked up with 1 tablespoonful of lemon juice and a pinch of salt, then stir this into the carrots, put the pan back on the fire, and stir just to bind the ingredients. It is ready as soon as the egg has cooked, which takes only a minute.

It is a good idea to serve with little squares of fried bread or toast.

Stuffed Tomatoes

For 6 people, choose 6 tomatoes of good size and make sure they are very clean. Cut in half horizontally, then scoop out the seedy central portions and drain off the juice so that each half is now transformed into a little red 'boat'. The filling is made by frying a sliced onion in 2 tablespoonfuls of olive oil and adding a chopped celery stick and parsley sprig, 4 ounces sliced mushrooms (if the mushrooms are dry, they must of course be soaked in warm water), salt, and pepper. Remove the pan from the stove, before adding 1 slice of soft white bread (not the crust) dipped in a little milk and squeezed out afterwards, 1 tablespoonful grated Parmesan, and an egg: the measures can be left rather vague (according to taste) so long as the paste is soft. Fill the tomato halves, then arrange them in a row in a baking dish greased with butter. Top each with a pat of butter and put into a moderate overn (350°F.) – not for long, because they mustn't split and run; 10–15 minutes is ample.

Artichokes alla Romana

Of all the ways of doing artichokes, I still prefer the classic *alla Romana,* which is quite different from the *alla Giudea.* The latter are deep-fried in a gigantic pan, and it is extremely difficult to cook them in the house. But for alla Romana artichokes all you do is follow instructions.

For 6 people buy 6 good plump artichokes, tear off the hard outside leaves and remove the chokes. Clip off the spiked leaf ends, soak artichokes in cold water to which you have added the juice of half a lemon to prevent them from going black. Meanwhile, chop 2 cloves of garlic and mix with 2 tablespoonfuls of chopped mint, about 4–6 ounces of soft white breadcrumbs, a sprinkling of salt and pepper and 2–3 tablespoonfuls of olive oil. Take the artichokes from their bath, dry off every drop of water very carefully, then very gently open the hearts and place a spoonful of the filling as deep in the heart of each artichoke as possible. Arrange artichokes upright, tightly packed in a baking dish, spoon about 1 tablespoonful olive oil over each artichoke, half cover them with cold water, sprinkle with pepper and salt, cover the dish and put in a moderate oven (about

375°F.). The artichokes will need an hour to cook. Now and then you should baste them with the juice in the bottom of the baking dish.

Fried Cauliflower all'Antica

Cook a 3-pound cauliflower in boiling water with very little salt until tender but still quite firm – al dente. Cut into pieces and fry in a pan with about 3 tablespoonfuls of olive oil and 2 already blanched cloves of garlic. When golden, add 2 tablespoonfuls of sultana raisins, 2 tablespoonfuls of pine nuts and a sprinkling of pepper and salt. Later on when the cooking is almost finished (it takes around 25 minutes altogether), add a handful of chopped parsley. Enough for 6 people.

Marrow in Egg Sauce

This is another old-fashioned recipe most undeservedly neglected these days, but I find it one of the best.

You must clean the vegetable marrow well – 2 pounds for 6 people – and cut into slices, then fry them in a pan with a little butter and a pinch of salt until golden brown. Keep them hot somewhere while you make the following sauce: beat up 3 eggs (one for 2 people) in the top of a double boiler with about 3 tablespoonfuls of softened butter, a pinch of salt and a pinch of cinnamon. This rather thick mixture is then diluted by adding 1 pint of light cold meat or chicken stock and a drop or two of vinegar; set over boiling water and stir steadily until the sauce thickens. Now it is ready. Put the marrow in a deep platter, sprinkle with grated cheese (Parmesan or Pecorino) and pour the sauce on top.

Stuffed Courgettes

The courgettes should be large and fairly chunky; plan on one for each person. First they are washed and dried, then cut in half lengthwise and the pulp scooped out, leaving shells about ¼-inch thick. You make the filling with 4 ounces minced beef, a slice of ham and a slice of mortadella sausage, all minced up together; add 1 slice of white bread trimmed of crusts, dipped in a little milk, then squeezed dry, then a tablespoonful of grated Parmesan, an egg, a pinch of salt, one of pepper, and one of nutmeg. Mix all into a paste and fill the courgette halves, piling the filling up. Arrange them in a tight row in a baking dish, and add about 1 tablespoonful each of olive oil and meat dripping (that is, if you have dripping; if not, just the oil). Bake uncovered in a moderate oven for about 1 hour until the vegetable is tender and the filling lightly browned.

Peas in Egg Sauce

In 1 tablespoonful olive oil fry 3 strips of lean bacon, diced, and 1 small chopped onion. Then add 1 pound of shelled fresh young green peas and continue cooking, adding several spoonfuls of water or stock if necessary to keep peas from sticking, and sprinkling lightly with pepper and salt. When the peas are nearly cooked, beat up 3 eggs in a bowl with 2 tablespoonfuls of fine dry breadcrumbs and 2 tablespoonfuls of grated Pecorino (if you can't find Pecorino, any cheese with a bite to it will do). Pour the egg mixture over the peas and stir very carefully. As soon as the egg begins to cook, the dish is ready. This amount will serve 4 amply.

Chicory and Bacon

Chicory is one of the nicest vegetables and the recipe I'm about to give you is a new one, which has only come into its own recently.

For 6 people you wash 6 good-sized heads scrupulously clean of all particles of earth. Cook them whole in a big pot of boiling water with only a little salt for about 10 minutes. When they are cooked (not overcooked because they mustn't lose their crispness), cut them in half, lengthwise. In the meantime heat 1 tablespoonful of olive oil in a pan with a couple of cloves of garlic which you must later remove. Now cut 2–3 strips of lean bacon into julienne strips or dice and fry them in the oil until crisp; then add the pieces of chicory sprinkling them with pepper and salt, and cook several minutes just until glazed.

Chicory and Anchovies

This is the original dish from which the chicory and bacon derives: chicory and anchovy.

Boil 6 heads for 10 minutes in lightly salted water, drain and cut lengthwise in half as in the previous recipe. Heat 2 tablespoonfuls of olive oil in a pan with 2 cloves of garlic peeled but not crushed, then take 3–4 fillets of anchovy, rinse off the salt, mince and fry them with a sprinkling of pepper. Wait for them to cook down into paste, then add the chicory and sprinkle lightly with salt and pepper: when the flavour has risen, add a few small leaves of mint before taking from the stove. Serves 6 people.

Asparagus and Cheese

We usually eat asparagus with a fried egg on top; or just the tips in soup. But here is a way of doing asparagus which has won many an Italian heart.

To start with, boil the asparagus according to the golden rule: i.e., in a bunch, upright with the heads peering over the surface of the boiling water (slightly salted) so that the tenderest parts will cook in the steam. When it is ready, separate the stalks and then make new smaller bundles (6 stalks in each) and wrap each bunch in a slice of soft cheese: Emmentaler or Fontina Valdostana is the best for the purpose. Grease a baking dish with butter, lay in the little bunches of asparagus, horizontally this time; put them in a hot oven (about 450°F.) just long enough for the cheese to get sticky without actually melting: the asparagus is ready. If you like, you might even pour a teaspoonful of tomato sauce on each bunch at serving time.

Broad Beans and Guanciale

This is a Roman dish which goes far back into ancient times. I do realize, of course, how hard it sometimes is to lay hands on the right ingredients, but I am so food-minded that it doesn't at all deter me from including it in my personal cuisine. At the same time I don't mind suggesting a variation or modification to simplify a complicated or difficult 'original'.

But broad beans will never be anything but broad beans. The Romans eat them raw with Pecorino cheese and I have difficulty finding them outside the area of Rome. (They are, of course, easy to come by in England.) *Guanciale* is very like bacon, but has a much more delicate taste as it really is made from pig's cheek, with the tenderest and sweetest fat on one side. If you do find broad beans, you'll need 2 pounds for 6 people. Shell the beans then cook them in a pan with a scant 4 ounces of guanciale cut into small pieces (as I said, failing guanciale, get the tenderest bacon you can find), add then 2 ounces of lard, or other fat and a spoonful of chopped onion (which has first been sautéed). Cook over a lively heat, stirring often and adding, if necessary, a few spoonfuls of water to keep the beans from sticking. Sprinkle with salt and pepper. When the beans are tender but still firm, they are done.

Peas and Ham

Sauté half a chopped onion in a pan with a scant 4 ounces of finely chopped salt pork; then add a pound of shelled very young tender green peas, a pinch of sugar, a sprinkling of pepper, and continue cooking, now and then pouring in a little stock, if necessary. When the peas are almost done, add 3 ounces of minced ham (including the fat) and cook a few minutes longer. This amount will serve 3–4 people.

Fennel in Vinegar Sauce

Heat about 3 tablespoonfuls of olive oil in a pan, then mash in it 3–4 anchovy fillets that have been rinsed free of salt and minced. This is a little sauce to cook your fennel in. Calculate one bulb of fennel per person, trim and scrub well, and cut into quarters. Add them to the pan, and as the fennel is cooking, sprinkle with pepper, then add about 7 ounces of white wine vinegar in which you have dissolved ⅛ teaspoonful of powdered mustard. Cover and continue cooking until the fennel is tender, about 15–20 minutes. At the end it might be a good idea to add a few drops of Tabasco.

Stuffed Potatoes

The potatoes should be big ones with firm flesh. Boil one per person, still in the skins, cut off one end and dig out the inside, leaving shells about ½ inch thick. (Whatever you do, don't remove the peel.) Then make the filling, which has many different formulas. My own is to put a few pieces of Mozzarella in each potato with the yolk of an egg, trying hard to get the yolk in without breaking it, a pinch of salt, more pieces of the cheese and a piece of anchovy. Then put back the ends you cut off so that the potatoes will look whole again, and pack them tightly in a baking dish. Put them in a hot oven for only a minute so that the Mozzarella begins to melt inside and bind the yolk.

Frizon

A big pan of vegetables is an honoured dish all through the land of Italy. In Emilia they call it frizon and that is what we are going to call it because I am following the recipe I learned near Parma.

Begin by putting plenty of good olive oil into a large pan, fry in it some sweet yellow, green, and red peppers cut into strips, then add a sliced onion (not too finely sliced) and some sliced courgettes. When these are cooking, drop in several cut-up tomatoes (you will have realized by now that a frizon doesn't fuss about with quantities; use your own judgment, since there is a bit of everything). Add a good sprinkling of pepper and salt, and cook until the various vegetables are reduced to a hodgepodge of pulp, each still retaining its original flavour.

VARIATION: You might even add a fresh sliced sausage to the frizon to cook along with it and heighten the taste of the vegetables. You will now have a really sumptuous feast as exciting to the palate as it is to the eye.

Emilian Grass Pie

In Emilia they call this pie *erbazzone* (or a pie made from assorted grasses) and in Lombardy *scarpazza* (which suggests a delicacy concocted from old shoes).

The real basis of the pie, however, is minced Swiss chard (or spinach, or fifty-fifty) with the addition of various ingredients. In Emilia they put a layer of pastry around it, while in Lombardy they do not. If you are going to make the pastry, you mix flour with a little dripping. For a pie for 6 people you would work 8 ounces of flour together with 4 ounces of lard or dripping and an occasional splash of water, just enough to hold the pastry together. This rolls out into a sheet of pastry which you use to line a shallow baking dish and to cover the pie. But first you must make the filling. You need 6 pounds of boiled Swiss chard or spinach, well drained of the water, and sautéed 10–15 minutes in a large pan with 2 ounces of chopped pork fat, the same quantity of butter and a chopped clove of garlic. Finally you mince the chard, then mix it with 3 lightly beaten eggs and 4 ounces of grated Parmesan. This is the 'grass' with which you fill the baking dish lined with the sheet of raw pastry. You then put on a top layer of the same dough, crimp and seal the edges and your pie is ready for the oven. Bake for 10 minutes in a hot oven (450°F.), then reduce heat to moderate (375°F.) and bake for 30 minutes longer.

It is delicious cut into slices even when it is cold. So it is the thing for parties and alfresco entertaining.

Lombardy Grass Pie

I have eaten practically the same pie in Lombardy, but without pastry. The difference is that the green vegetable – Swiss chard or spinach – prepared as I have described down to the addition of the beaten eggs, is seasoned with a handful of sultanas, another of pine nuts, a pinch of cinnamon and 4 ounces of crushed biscuits (the sort you eat with cheese, not sweet biscuits). You put the mixture into a well-buttered baking dish dusted with breadcrumbs and on top you sprinkle more breadcrumbs, dot with a few pats of butter and consign to a moderate oven (350°F.) for about half an hour.

Parmigiana

This is a truly magnificent dish, and at the same time an unfathomable mystery to me. Why Parmigiana if it is a dish that is not only as Neapolitan as San' Gennaro, but one of the proudest monuments of Naples cuisine? Historical injustice? Involuntary error? Or a conspiracy? In any case here is what it is made of:

Clean and slice some large aubergines, say 2 pounds for 6 people. Each slice should be a little less than ¼ inch thick. Place slices on a large plate, cover with coarse salt, then cover with another plate and weight it with something heavy so that the slices extrude their bitter juices. After a couple of hours, wash and dry the slices and squeeze them a little, very gently, to get them as dry as possible. Then fry them in plenty of hot olive oil.

Make a sauce with tomatoes (say under 2 pounds, or slightly less than the weight of the aubergine), peel, chop and sieve them; put them in the pan with a pinch of salt and a few basil leaves, but without oil; you only have to wait for a little of the tomato juice to reduce before the sauce starts to thicken. At this point you put a few spoonfuls of the sauce into an oiled baking dish, then a layer of fried aubergine, then sprinkle with grated Parmesan, then put down a layer of thinly sliced Mozzarella with a few leaves of basil, and a spoonful of beaten egg. Begin all over again with the sauce, the aubergine, the Parmesan, Mozzarella, egg, and back to home base, so that you end up with at least three layers of everything. Bake uncovered in a hot oven (425°F.) for 40–50 minutes.

VARIATIONS on this dish, which is reverenced throughout the length and breadth of Italy, include one with the aubergine dipped in egg and flour before frying; so that the taste is more delicate. It can also be made with half aubergine and half courgette, which is more delicate still.

Mushrooms with Vine Leaves

This is an incredibly bright idea which I learned in Liguria, the region around Genoa.

You need large, fleshy mushrooms, the white, egg-shaped ones, or the huge *porcini*. Cut off the stem, then make a light incision in the shape of a cross underneath the hat; sprinkle each one with a few drops of olive oil to which you have added a pinch of salt, one of pepper, and a spoonful of chopped parsley. Then prepare the open grill. Beneath it you should not only have wood or charcoal but a thin layer of vine leaves. Cook the mushrooms over this, upside down, i.e. the bottoms up. As the fire burns, the vine leaves give off a delicious heady aroma, which permeates the mushrooms. So that is all you will need.

Stuffed Mushrooms

Here you will want fleshy, medium-sized mushrooms. Clean them and twist out the stems, then give the 'hats' the lightest possible dusting of salt. Stuff each of the mushrooms with a mixture of eggs beaten with 2 tablespoonfuls of grated Parmesan, a pinch of chopped parsley, and a little chopped garlic. With this, you can stuff quite a few mushrooms because you won't need more than a teaspoonful for each. Once they are filled, sauté them in olive oil in a pan over a high flame, just until golden. When the moment comes for serving, add a few dabs of butter and more chopped parsley.

Parmesan Pie with Truffles

If you love Parmesan cheese and love truffles too, you will realize that this can be quite a vitalizing gastronomic experience.

Grease a baking dish with butter and put down a layer of white truffles, cut into thin slices; on the truffles, a layer of little squares of Parmesan; then another layer of truffles and another of Parmesan. You can build up to three layers of each if the idea attracts you. Douse everything in olive oil, put in a hot oven for a few minutes, just enough time for the cheese to soften and bind the truffles.

If this sounds a bit heavy, you could modify like this: make a polenta and shape a good circle out of it (between ¼- and ½-inch thick), as the first layer in the baking dish. Then using it as a base, start building your layers of Parmesan and truffles. I find the pie even nicer this way.

Boiled Potatoes

Not everybody realizes it, but few vegetables make such an excellent accompaniment for sauce dishes as plain old boiled potatoes. They are also good as a salad dressed with oil, vinegar, and parsley. But this way of seasoning them can be vastly improved by a method much in use in rural districts of Italy. It doesn't sound much in the telling: but I can assure you it has a magic touch.

Boil the potatoes, as usual, then peel, cut them into average slices, not too thick and not too thin. Mix some olive oil and vinegar, twice as much oil as vinegar, and heat in a little saucepan; then add a handful of chopped parsley and one or two minutely chopped cloves of garlic. (You *can* do without garlic, if you like; but it would be a shame.) When it is hot, pour it on the potatoes. What did I say? Isn't it the easiest thing in the world? But you can't imagine how brilliant that potato salad is going to taste!

DIGRESSION
(My husband, the involtino*)*

In the course of some interviews with writers and journalists who were writing my life story, I often found myself talking about an old and harmless mania of mine: that of giving all the people I love or who interest me a nickname, the name of some kind of food. For many years now, I have been calling my husband, Carlo Ponti, *involtino* (and in the pages of this book, you will see just how fond I am of this dish!). But among my friends and in unexpected meetings with new people, for some reason I suddenly associate them with food. As it invariably happens with people I like, and calling them *fettuccine* or *cannolicchi* or *frittata* has a positive meaning, my interviewers have often come up with an interpretation which fringes on the psychoanalytical.

One explanation which I find the truest is that in my earliest childhood during the war, the privations which we suffered at the time must have inculcated in me an absolute respect for the food which was so difficult to find in those years.

All the stages of my life and my career have been marked by my urgent desire for protection and security. I have had to fight hard, especially in my private life, but each time I have won, and it has never been a case of sheer caprice or foolish illusions. Food for me is a symbol of security, just as is the roof that shelters me. So it is a symbol which has become sacred.

If one day you meet me, whether it is at the shop, or crushed elbow to elbow at some cocktail party, or working on the set, and if I suddenly call you 'potato chip' or 'stuffed turkey' or any dish at all, remember what I have written in these pages and you will realize I have taken an immediate fancy to you.

Sweets

These days, I know, very few people make sweets at home. It is so much more practical to buy them ready-made. It isn't just the tremendous saving of time and effort, but the fact that the bakers' shops and confectioners are so much better equipped for the job. But I still love the idea of making a cake or a sweet with my own hands. It is something that lies in the heart and home, with the warmth of friendship and affection. Being able to say to someone: 'I made this cake or this pudding myself. I made it for you because I know it's your favourite.' Isn't that the real way of showing love and affection? Certainly more than handing over a gift or running down to buy a commercial *cassata* in the shop around the corner. And how often an awkward moment, a strain, can be charmingly got over by a simple little gesture.

But more than anything there is the fun of messing around with sugar, vanilla, and whipped cream. I find it relaxing. Never fail to do it, for example, before having friends in for tea or, and here it is still more effective, before sitting down with them to a game of poker.

Snow Eggs

Break 6 eggs, separating the yolks from the whites; beat the whites with a whisk, adding a pinch of salt and about 3 ounces of sugar. Continue whisking until the mixture is almost solid. Meanwhile, have 1 quart of milk heating in a large saucepan. When the milk comes to the boil, add the stiffly beaten whites, spoonful after spoonful.

You'll see these snow eggs will form at once and when you scoop them gently out with a perforated spoon, they will be light as snow but each in one compact piece. Arrange them in a serving dish, cover with a cream which you will easily make with the milk left over in the saucepan and the yolks of the eggs which you put aside. You simply beat the yolks with about 4 ounces of sugar, stir in a little hot milk, then return to the pan and heat and stir over low heat 1–2 minutes until slightly thickened. You may even add a liqueur glass of cognac.

Chocolate Mousse

I have a confession. This is my favourite sweet and my very worst enemy as regards diet. I only have to see it and all my resistance melts - like a teenager in the clutches of a professional seducer.

I start out by making the classic English custard. I boil 1 quart of milk with 8 ounces of sugar and half a vanilla bean in the top of a double boiler but over direct heat. Then I take it off the heat and add 10 beaten egg yolks, mixed first with a few tablespoonfuls of the hot milk. Then I set it over boiling water and keep stirring and whisking the mixture until the custard begins to thicken. Then it's off the fire again and into a cool spot for about an hour. Now we have the classic custard. For its final transformation I add 1½ pints of heavy cream, whipped until stiff, and a few teaspoonfuls of unsweetened cocoa; then I beat them together well away from the heat (in the kitchens of the great chefs, this operation is actually done on a block of ice) until the mixture becomes frothy. This is the chocolate mousse. Pour it into a glass bowl and chill well in the refrigerator. This will serve 6–8 people.

Bavarian Pudding Italian Style

Bavarian pudding is well known all over Italy, much more than in southern Germany. One Italian version was consecrated by the most famous Italian writer on cookery, almost a century ago, Pellegrino Artusi. There are also other versions. This is the one I know.

Boil 6 eggs until they are almost hard-boiled, but not quite. Shell them, scoop out the yolks, beat them up with 4 ounces of butter, then pass it all through the sieve, adding 6 ounces of sugar and a teaspoonful of vanilla; stir steadily then add 2 or 3 tablespoonfuls of roughly chopped walnuts, and mix again until it becomes a smoothly blended paste. Then take a mould and moisten it with rum. Open a package of sponge fingers and dip half of them in rum, and the other half in cherry brandy. Alternately with sponge fingers from both piles line the bottom and sides of the mould. Then pour in the mixture, cover with more rum-and-cherry brandy sponge fingers. Then leave it to stand for a few hours in the refrigerator.

Candied Almonds

Of all the almond sweets made in Italy this must be the most popular. And it couldn't be easier, if you have a copper cooking pot with a rounded base.

Blanch and skin 2 pounds of almonds, then put them in a slow oven to dry out. Meanwhile heat in the copper pot 2 pounds of sugar and about ½ pint of water, just enough to melt the sugar. When the sugar begins to acquire a reddish tinge pour in the almonds; mix and stir over a moderate heat until the sugar begins to look rather sandy. You must continue the cooking so that the sugar caramelizes and coats the almonds. Then pour the whole mixture on to a marble-topped table, slightly greased, and allow it to cool, before breaking into pieces.

Quite a treat in the way of variation is that when pouring the almonds into the pan, you also add a little melted bitter chocolate.

Pumpkin Pie

I love all pies, and especially American pumpkin pie, for the simple reason that it is made out of pumpkin. You want the big sweet pumpkin we have here in Italy, particularly in the Po Valley, where I learned so many of my recipes. Now I'll tell you how I make the pie, and hope I get it all right.

Sift 4 ounces of white flour already mixed with ½ teaspoonful of salt; then add a tablespoonful of butter and 2 of lard already blended together (if you can't get lard or dripping, some other fat will do). Work it with your hands with the aid of 1 or 2 tablespoonfuls of warm water and eventually roll out a sheet of pastry, fairly – but not too – thin. This is your lining for an 8-inch pie pan.

Now for the filling: boil ½ pint of milk, take off the heat and add 2 tablespoonfuls of butter, 2 egg yolks beaten with a little of the hot milk, 4 ounces of sugar, a teaspoonful of cinnamon, ¼ teaspoonful of nutmeg, ¼ teaspoonful of cloves, a pinch of salt, and a pinch of ginger. These should then all be mixed in a bowl with 8 ounces of pumpkin purée (pumpkin should first be baked in sections, then puréed). Mix with a cane beater, if possible, rather than a metal one. When the mixture has become light and foamy, finish off by folding in 2 stiffly beaten whites of egg; continue to stir hard, then pour the filling into the pastry and put it in a hot oven (450°F.) for 10 minutes; reduce heat to moderate (375°F.) and bake for another half-hour. Serve tepid but not hot. A topping of whipped cream would go down brilliantly.

Bocconotti

This sweet, again, belongs to the inexhaustible treasure house of my own Naples, and southern Italy.

You make a sweet pastry dough with 1 pound of flour, 3 tablespoonfuls of sugar and as much water as you need to get the dough soft and consistent. (To improve the pastry some people add 2 or 3 tablespoonfuls of oil.) Roll the pastry thin (but not too thin) then cut into discs 2 or 3 inches in diameter. On each disc place a small dab of black cherry jam or quince jelly; fold over the edges of the disc to cover the jam and press them well together, into a half-moon. Then you brush these bocconotti with beaten yolk of egg and bake them in a hot oven (425°F.) for 20 minutes.

VARIATION: you can fill half the bocconotti with jam and the other half with a crème (or custard) used for pastry.

Ricotta Pie

For the base you must bake a *pasta frolla* (soft, sweet pastry) to cover with with a filling of ricotta (Italian cottage cheese) and other ingredients. The pasta frolla is made by mixing 8 ounces (scant) of sifted flour, 3½ ounces of butter, 4 ounces (scant) of sugar, an egg and an egg yolk, a large pinch of salt, and a little grated lemon rind. It must not be beaten or stirred too much otherwise it will become too elastic. If it tends to disintegrate, you can knead it better by adding a little cold water. Then let it stand wrapped in a linen cloth for about an hour.

Meanwhile mix up in a bowl a pound of ricotta, 8 ounces (scant) of sugar, an egg and two yolks, 2 tablespoonfuls of sultanas, 2 of pine nuts, grated lemon rind, some diced candied orange and citron peel (all measurements to your personal taste; it won't make any difference to a ricotta pie if you use more or less citron, or pine nuts, or sultanas), but it is important to see that all ingredients are well distributed.

Finally cut the pasta frolla in two to make two little sheets of pastry. The first serves to line the bottom and sides of a pie dish greased with butter; into it you spoon the ricotta filling. Then you put the other sheet of pastry on top, cut into strips which you arrange criss-cross, as in all pies of this sort. There will of course be left-overs from this second sheet, which you can use to make a border around the edge of the pie dish. Brush the border and the criss-cross pastry across the top with beaten egg, then place in a medium oven (375°F.) for 30 minutes. Serve cold, dusted with icing sugar.

Orange Ricotta Tarts

This Sicilian sweet is a very simple variation on the theme of cassata, cannoli, and so on.

Mix the ricotta with sugar, candied orange and citron peel. For 2 pounds of ricotta you will need about 8 ounces of sugar and about 4 ounces of chopped candied fruits. This is your filling for little tarts made from pasta frolla (see recipe for Strawberry Tart), which you will have already prepared and baked. If you don't feel up to making the pasta frolla, you can always buy a packet of mixed biscuits, or a *pan di Spagna* (a plain, fairly dry sponge cake). One last touch: cover each ricotta tart with fresh grated orange rind. Simple, you see, but delicious and beautiful on the plate.

Ricotta

Roman ricotta which is so delicate and so full of flavour is the basis of many sweet dishes apart from the pie and tarts I have just given you. It is also very good on its own, or with the addition of one or two flavours. For example, here is how I served it to Peter Sellers the first time he came to my house in Marino, near Rome. Peter was completely bowled over and now every time he comes to see us the first thing he does is to shout for his ricotta.

Put about a pound of ricotta (or cottage cheese) in a bowl. Pour over it 3 or 4 tablespoonfuls of sugar (more if you have a sweet tooth). Not too much, mind. Then the same quantity of bitter cocoa and a couple of liqueur glasses of cognac; stir well and serve.

VARIATIONS: Mix the ricotta with sugar and cinnamon; or with sugar, cinnamon and a strongly flavoured liqueur: Framboise or Cointreau, for example; or you can mix it with sugar, finely ground coffee beans and cognac.

Apple Fritters alla Romana

Apple fritters are always a treat. But as I love the Roman ones, I want to give you the recipe.

The apples should be plump, firm, and crisp. Core them, peel them, slice them and put them into a bowl, adding sugar and a liqueur (Anise, for example), and let them absorb the flavours for half an hour. Meanwhile prepare the batter: for 2 pounds of apples you will want 8 ounces of flour mixed with 2 tablespoonfuls melted butter, 1 pint of cold water, a tablespoonful of the same liqueur the apples are macerating in, and a pinch of salt. Finally, mix in 2 whites of egg whisked into a stiff snow. Use the batter at once by dipping in the slices of apple, patted very dry on paper towelling, then dropping them into a pot of hot oil. As soon as each fritter becomes golden and crisp, remove it from the pan, drain on absorbent paper and dust with icing sugar. Serve very hot.

Apple Cake

Mix 1 pound of sugar with just under a pint of cold water in a large saucepan and bring to the boil. Meanwhile, clean and peel 2½ pounds of apples, cut into slices a little less than ¼-inch thick (after removing the cores, add the sliced apples to the syrup in the saucepan, and cook very slowly over a mild flame, giving an occasional, but very gentle, stir. When they are soft and the mixture thick, add the grated rind of a lemon (avoiding of course the pith), 2 ounces of minced candied orange peel and 2 ounces of minced candied citron. Stir for the last time, then remove from the fire. Pour the mixture into a mould, cool, then refrigerate for a few hours. When the time comes to serve, put the mould in boiling water for a few seconds and then turn it upside down: tip out your apple cake and serve under a good sprinkling of Kirsch or black cherry syrup.

Strawberry Tart

Make a pasta frolla with 7 ounces of flour, 7 ounces of butter, 7 ounces of sugar, a whole egg plus the yolk of another, a pinch of salt, and the grated rind of half a lemon. Mix well but not too enthusiastically, adding water only if you see that the dough tends to crumble. Then leave it to stand in a linen cloth somewhere in the open. When it has settled, roll it into a sheet of pastry and use it to line a 9- or 10-inch pie dish greased with butter, bake 5 minutes in a very hot oven (475–500°F.), then lower heat to moderate (375°F.) and bake about 10 minutes more until crisp and golden. As I was able to discover (by poking my nose around some of the most famous restaurants in France), this tart has its pastry cooked separately. (So you must make quite sure that the empty pastry doesn't rise in the middle. Do this by adding some uncooked rice or dried beans, which you remove afterwards and save for another time.)

Now that you have your case of pastry, crisp and

golden brown inside and out, add a layer first of all of blackcurrant jelly, then arrange the strawberries in the jelly. The little wood strawberries are the best, as they have the most flavour. If you like, serve with a topping of whipped cream.

Raspberry Tart

Make a sheet of pastry with 7 ounces of flour, 3½ ounces of butter, 4 ounces of sugar, the yolk of an egg, a pinch of salt and one of cinnamon. Roll out and line a 9-inch pie dish with the pastry and bake 5 minutes in a hot oven (450°F.), lower heat to moderate (375°F.), and bake 10–15 minutes more. Now you have the pastry baked and ready for your tart.

For the filling: scald 1 pint of milk with 3 ounces of sugar and half a vanilla bean; beat 3 eggs with a tablespoonful of sugar; and add a little of the vanilla milk to the eggs, then stir all into the milk remaining in the pan. Mix well, and when custard has cooled almost to room temperature, pour over the bottom of the tart; then arrange a layer of raspberries over the custard and sprinkle with sugar; finally you top with 2 egg whites, beaten to 'snow' with 2 tablespoonfuls of sugar. Leave in a hot oven just long enough for the meringue to be dappled with gold, then serve.

Chestnut Roll

The chestnuts (a pound, say) must first be roasted, then shelled, and cooked with 4 ounces (scant) of sugar, half a stick of vanilla and enough milk to cover them. When they are quite soft, strain out the chestnuts, put them through a fine sieve. Flavour with a little liqueur (I leave the choice to you but recommend Kirsch or apricot brandy). Finally on a sheet of waxed paper shape the purée into a disc, ⅛-inch thick. Over the disc spread another layer, slightly smaller in diameter, of jam (best of all if you use jam of the same fruit as the liqueur). Now roll the double disc up in the waxed paper and let it stand. At the time of serving remove the paper and cut the roll into slices. On each slice you can put a dollop of whipped cream.

Fried Magnolia Petals

This probably summons up visions of Sheherazade, but it comes down to us from the classic tradition of Renaissance cooking. In certain parts of Italy, it is still served at extremely elegant dinners. The petals, I am here to tell you, are sublime. The only trouble is finding them. In my house at Marino, in the Roman hills, there are three gigantic magnolia trees in the garden outside the front door. On the early summer evenings their scent wafts through my bedroom windows, with their message of golden sunshine in a creamy blue sky. There are so many magnolia flowers to choose from on the trees, but I normally pick the ones with fleshier, softer petals. Here is how I deal with them in the kitchen.

Make a little batter with 3½ ounces of flour, 2 whites of egg and 3 ounces of sugar. Dip the petals so that both sides are covered, but without dropping them in; fry them in plenty of oil until golden and crisp. Then drain on porous paper and sprinkle with sugar. They will come as a brilliant surprise for your dinner guests.

VARIATIONS: Instead of magnolia petals, you can cook orange blossoms in the same way or acacia flowers or violets.

Banana Boats

Slit open some largish ripe bananas down one side, cut away a strip of the skin, just enough to remove the pulp without damaging the rest which has now acquired the shape of a canoe. For 6 people you will need 6 bananas; mash the pulp in a bowl, adding 3 tablespoonfuls of sugar, a good pinch of cinnamon, a little glass of rum (or more if you like rum). Then let it stand somewhere to keep cool. Meanwhile, in another bowl, mix about 6 ounces of shredded coconut with 2 tablespoonfuls of sugar and 2 stiffly whisked whites of egg. When all the ingredients are blended, mix in the banana mixture and blend everything with the lightest touch. With this you fill the banana 'boats' (which should be well washed). Set them in a baking dish greased with butter and leave them for 10 minutes in a moderate oven (375°F.). Then remove them from the oven, douse with rum, set them alight and serve.

Melon with Strawberries

Plan on one small melon per person. Slice off the top, the stem end, and very carefully scoop out the seeds and flesh; dice the flesh (or else scoop into little balls with the correct instrument); replace a part of the dice (or balls) in each melon, sprinkle with sugar; then over them add a layer of wood strawberries (or large strawberries cut small), which you then moisten with a few drops of lemon juice. Carry on like this, alternating the layers of melon, sugar, wood strawberries, and lemon juice. Finally you pour in a dash of cognac or white rum, or a cherry or apricot liqueur. Put the 'lid' back on each melon (i.e. the top you cut off at the beginning). Leave in the refrigerator until it is time to serve.

Gelu 'I Muluni
(Watermelon Ice)

This is an enchanting Sicilian sweet. A particular summer favourite in Palermo.

You cut out the flesh of a perfectly ripened watermelon. Sieve it and put it in a large saucepan (you should have about 3 pints of seeded, chopped watermelon) with 1 lb. 8 oz. of sugar, and 3 envelopes of gelatine previously softened in ¼ pint cold water; mix well, and boil for a few minutes. When you have taken it from the fire, add ½ teaspoonful of vanilla, then 6 ounces of chocolate chips cut in half, 3 tablespoonfuls each of minced candied orange rind and citron, about 4 ounces of blanched, coarsely chopped pistachios. Keep stirring so that everything is distributed uniformly; then pour into a mould and keep in the refrigerator for at least 3 hours.

Sweet Tarallucci

Tarallucci are doughnuts. In Naples they instantly conjure up visions of *feste* and celebrations, and there is a popular expression for anything that has turned out particularly well. They say, 'Everything has ended up *tarallucci e vino,'* to great rejoicing all round.

Tarallucci are made by mixing in a bowl 3 eggs, a tablespoonful of sugar and one of liqueur (a fruit eau-de-vie such as Kirsch or Slivovitz); then add 10 ounces (scant) of flour, working them all into a dough, then add ½ teaspoonful of vanilla and ½ teaspoonful of powdered cinnamon. The mixture, which should be finely blended and consistent, is cut into strips, joined at the end to form doughnuts, then fried carefully in plenty of hot oil. A word of advice: to get the best out of your tarallucci, take them out of the oil when they are half cooked, then make an incision right around the ring with a knife before dropping them back in the oil. When they are cooked, they should be thoroughly drained on porous paper. And remember, they are even better when eaten cold.

Zabaione

In Italy, and especially in the south, they have the amusing custom of offering newlyweds, whenever they happen to be invited, a good stiff zabaione. The implication being that the young bride and groom will need all the strength they can get as they put their backs into the first days of wedlock. That is why one of the sights of Italy is to observe some young blood in the local bar loudly order a zabaione then look proudly around to make sure everyone realizes he is just back from a session in bed. Most likely it won't be true; he will only be doing it to keep his spirits up – but the fact remains that zabaione is considered a powerful collaborator in the act of love.

The best way of making it, to my mind, is in a double

boiler. Put 6 egg yolks in the top with 6 tablespoonfuls of sugar and less than a tablespoonful of water. Stir these ingredients over simmering water. The mixture soon acquires a smooth consistency; now add a wineglass of sweet marsala, not all at once, just a little at a time as you keep stirring vigorously. Now whisk it into a pale golden froth. Some people add a pinch of cinnamon with the marsala, which I think goes wonderfully well. Zabaione is delicious served with a few slices of pan di Spagna (sponge cake). But why say more? It is such a beautiful sweet, it would be a sensation with almost anything. This amount will serve 6 people.

INDEX